Other works by Brian Baleno

<u>Novels</u>
+ One

<u>Non-Fiction</u>
Fifty Halfs from First to Last
Generational Lessons from Dad

<u>Poetry</u>
Forgotten Shoebox Poems & Photos

D1528798

Insignificant Ones

Brian Baleno

Dedication

For my significant ones

Contents

Acknowledgments

Copyeditor: Martin Ceisel
Proofreader: Jeff Rudolph
Reviewer: Lauren Bennett
Reviewer: Kim Palaza
Cover Art: Martha Whidden
Beta Reader: Mary DeSantis
Beta Reader: Nicole Mentges
Beta Reader: Char Jones
Beta Reader: Rachel Swords

FRIDAY

If tomorrow is better than today, then tomorrow will be a great day. Today is Friday, and not just any typical Friday where under normal circumstances, I would be counting the hours until my weekend begins. I just received a text message from my fiancée informing me that she has been charged with insider trading. That's right, a text message—not a phone call or even an email. How could she send me a text for a felony charge? I can understand sending your future spouse a text informing them of a $20 parking ticket, but not a charge that could result in federal prison time. Even a misdemeanor merits a phone call.

When did our law system move from getting a single phone call to allowing three text messages? I guess I missed that memo, or maybe I am a bit old fashioned. I've always been a bit of an old soul, steeped in conventions of yesteryear, so the migration of phone calls to texts has always been a pet peeve of mine. One could count the number of text messages I send and receive in a week on one hand. What can I say? I'm a poor thumb communicator.

To make things worse, her ex-boyfriend and colleague, Jack, was also charged in the conspiracy. I never liked Jack and I'm sure he is not very fond of me either. The two of us have absolutely nothing in common outside of being in love with Lana, either presently, or hopefully in the past for Jack.

The minute hand on my watch seemed to be frozen in time while the second hand indicated that my blue-and-white faced Vaer functioned as it should. The watch was an engagement gift from Lana and the first watch I ever owned worth more than fifty dollars. I desperately wanted to escape the confines of my 48-square-foot cubicle to contact Lana. I glanced across the span of the eighth-floor sports writers' offices, seeking to discover who among my colleagues was still working. All the senior writers whose cubes were on the outside of the perimeter of the office had pretty much called it quits for the week. I aspired one day to move up the cubicle ladder to a desk in front of the floor-to-ceiling windows that overlooked Piedmont Park. On any other Friday I may start daydreaming as the last few working minutes of the day expire, but not today. Today all my attention was centered on Lana's predicament.

There was no possible scenario in which my beautiful fiancée would do something so abominable. My thoughts drifted toward unthinkable scenes. I started to picture Lana with her long thick dark brown hair and her deep espresso eyes sitting on a steel bench in a jail cell surrounded by hardened criminals. I could not fathom Lana with her petite frame sitting next to an armed robber who had spent the last ten years pumping iron. Imagining her in that white and orange prison attire was just too much.

What had transpired at Lana's law firm? Are the charges legitimate? Could she merely be a victim in a business deal gone wrong? The questions continued to compile in my mind. I wished that life provided a window into our future. I would be happy with a mere glimpse. *Stay tuned for scenes from next week's episode*, said the voice in my head. Unfortunately, or maybe fortunately, we never get a glimpse of what our lives have in store for us. The best we can do is make educated directional decisions that lead to our desired outcome. Even then, the outcomes are completely unpredictable.

Lana's being charged with insider trading.

Case in point.

I avoided the urge to Google Lana's name. There had to be an explanation. Two hours earlier, my editor applauded my latest article breaking the news of a blockbuster trade between the Atlanta Braves and Pittsburgh Pirates. Tomorrow, it could be possible that my fiancée's name will appear in the business section of the very newspaper that employs me. I wondered if the news of her charge was substantial enough for local journalists to cover. At this point, I was failing to imagine how tomorrow could be better than today. The only way that would be possible is if this was all a bad dream.

The two matters that could not escape me were the charge against Lana and the involvement of Jack, her ex-boyfriend. What puzzled me the most was the idea that Lana would be involved in any type of criminal activity. I had never known someone to be as honest and have as much integrity as Lana. I had once witnessed Lana correct the salesclerk at Brooks Brothers when she recognized that he had undercharged her for the shirt she was purchasing, among other things.

Aside from her principled ethics, she valued her career and the firm she worked for. There was no way she would jeopardize the company she worked for. Lana embodies good ethics. Additionally, she has dedicated so much time to pursuing her law degree and practicing law that she would not risk being disbarred. She had too much going for her. She loved her job, despite the stress that came with eighty-hour work weeks. By no means was she a risk taker or gambler. To the contrary, when we traveled to Las Vegas for a conference a few years ago, she refused to even play the quarter slots. Things were not adding up.

At half past five, I packed up my laptop and drove home to Buckhead. Interstate 85 was a parking lot, which only heightened my frustration. I could barely hear my phone ring with the blaring horns around me. Lana's name appeared on the car's infotainment screen.

"Hey baby, how are you? Are you home yet?"

"Matty, I'm home now, but I'm leaving in ten minutes to meet with my attorney. It's been a horrible day and I don't have the energy right now to get into the details."

"Do you want me to meet you there?"

"No, it's better that I go alone. I don't want you involved in this."

"Lana, how did all of this start? Was your firm working on a deal with the company?"

"Yes, they were a client of ours."

"You're not guilty though, right?"

"No. Everything I did was completely legal. Please do not worry. It will all work itself out."

"Are you sure you don't want me to go with you to meet the lawyer?"

"Yes. It's going to take a while, so you should give the guys a call and meet them for a drink."

"I'd rather spend the night with you."

"I'll see you later tonight. Just go to dinner without me and we'll meet later."

I was confused and frustrated. All I wanted to do was to be there for Lana. At the same time, I had learned over the past several years when to give her the space she needed. She would never achieve the title for great communicator. She was no

Steve Jobs or Elon Musk. Feelings and emotions were only to be discussed on Lana's terms—a rare and infrequent event.

Eddie was sitting on the couch talking on his phone when I opened the condo door. Honey, my four-year-old golden retriever raced to the door to greet me. I motioned to him that I wanted to talk, and he responded by lifting his pointer finger indicating to wait a minute. I proceeded to my bedroom, dropping my laptop bag on my bed. A rainstorm ensued, and hail started to strike the windows. I walked to the end of the room and stared out at the gray Atlanta skyline.

Back in the living room, Eddie was still on the phone. He lifted his eyebrows and shrugged his shoulders as if to say, *I am trying to get off the phone but can't.* At this point, I was so consumed with anxiety that I quickly changed clothes and decided to go for a run. Like usual, Honey was anxious to accompany me. She is my best running buddy, which is why I felt guilty looking down as Honey patiently stared at me with her tail wagging. "Treadmill, today, sweetie." Running indoors on the 10th floor overlooking the Atlanta skyline was much better than getting pelted with hail and having a soaking wet dog. Eddie gave me the thumbs up as I was leaving.

When I returned, Eddie was nowhere to be seen. Honey looked up at me with her sad brown eyes.

Eddie is a complete neat freak, so it took an enormous amount of effort and energy convincing him that I would keep Honey and the condo clean. That promise, as well as the purchase of a Roomba vacuum to account for Honey's consistent shedding. Still, Honey followed me into my bedroom and rested her snout on my leg as I sat down on the ottoman in front of my bed. I reached for my phone to check if Lana had called or texted. Nothing. Still tied up with the lawyers, I guessed. I desperately needed someone to talk to about this all.

Where was Eddie? I called him, but my call went straight to voicemail.

Like Lana and Jack, Eddie also practiced law. He worked as a corporate attorney for a large IT company, while Lana and Jack were corporate attorneys working for the same Atlanta law firm, specializing in mergers and acquisitions. Eddie had met Lana at University of Georgia law school in Athens. My alma mater—though not for law, which is part of the reason we three never crossed paths until well after graduation.

As it turns out, we'd both relocated to Atlanta, Eddie after finishing his law degree, myself after earning a master's in journalism. Gosh, that unpaid internship at the *New Atlanta Times* was a drag. But after a year of interning, they hired me as a junior beat writer working sports. With my new job and steady income in hand, I began searching for a roommate. I soon found Eddie's Craigslist ad and moved into his two-bedroom condo in Buckhead, where we've lived together ever since.

Sometimes the stars enter our orbit unexpectedly, while others have always been there forever, but for some reason go unnoticed. Luckily for me, the brightest star in my orbit, Lana, happened to live in the same Eclipse condo building as Eddie. Looking back, it really was a perfect collision; but if not for Honey, I'm not sure that we would have ever spoken to one another. The love-at-first-sight moment for Honey and me occurred when Lana first entered the elevator. As the elevator began to descend, neither of us attempted to make eye contact with the other. Honey happily wagged her tail and whimpered as we slowly approached the bottom floor, at which point Lana asked me if she could pet her. Our eyes locked and that was it for me. By the time we reached ground level, I had invited Lana to join Honey and I on our walk.

I always considered golden retrievers to be the Brad Pitt of dogs, and the Lana-and-Honey encounter proves my point. Dogs are like magnets, the way they draw people to them. I immediately knew that Lana was out of my league, of course. In this case, I had outkicked my punt coverage team. With long thick dark brown hair and delicate facial features, Lana's natural beauty intimidated me. Not only was she beautiful, but she also dressed like a real working professional. Compared to my old worn-out untied navy Toms, tattered jeans, and faded tee, we looked like complete opposites.

Of course, the intimidation was purely physical at first. How could this beautiful girl be attracted to a wiry runner who hardly owned a single pair of "nice" shoes. My work attire was no more impressive, with faded khaki pants and a sports coat needed for the more formal events I had to attend. I could not even fathom a guess where someone like her shopped for skirts and blouses and whatever other type of luxury garments a young upwardly mobile lawyer would wear. My insecurity compounded after I learned that she graduated at the top of her class from both Georgia Tech and UGA. Brilliant. Beautiful. I was in awe.

It wasn't until I attended one of Lana's company's holiday parties that I learned why Lana was attracted to me. My lack of polish and confidence had to be obvious to not only Lana, but also her peers and their respective spouses. From the moment I entered the lavish gala, a word that only became part of my vocabulary after meeting Lana, I felt utterly awkward and inadequate. Events like these were a rare form of torture that led to intense anxiety and stress. Couple that with the fact that Lana's ex-boyfriend and colleague Jack would be in attendance, and . . .

Shoot. I just never quite meshed well with people who articulated themselves so smoothly. Lawyers and politicians innately glide through conversations, passing from one person to the next with ease. I envied those types, who seemed to possess the ability to approach complete strangers and break the ice with ease

Growing up in a middle-class Pittsburgh suburb, I never developed the sophisticated social skills to communicate with the intellectual elites. I lacked the Ivy League pedigree and always felt like a fish out of water when I encountered those of enormous wealth, power, and influence. As the son of a general contractor and homemaker, my family had no formal association with the social class that belongs to country clubs, attends local theater and opera productions, or has access to the luxury boxes in stadiums and arenas. Ironically, years later my profession would provide me with daily access to Major League ball players. Never in a million years would I have thought that I would be a regular in the dugout, clubhouse, and training facilities of professional baseball teams.

My minimal cultural awareness stemmed from occasional school field trips to downtown Pittsburgh. During these excursions, our class ventured into the cultural district where we learned about the philanthropic gestures of famous Pittsburgh industrialists. We grew to understand the history of Andrew Carnegie, Henry John Heinz, and Andrew Mellon. Our teachers paired the entrepreneurial achievements of steel production, food condiments like ketchup and mustard, and finance with the generosity of these families in giving back to the city of Pittsburgh. Each successful family chose their own philanthropic pursuit which has transcended time, extending into the present day. Carnegie Mellon University, Heinz Hall for the Performing Arts, and Heinz Memorial Chapel come to mind, all of it seemingly far away from my little corner of Pennsylvania.

The sparse social etiquette I acquired came from my cinematic viewing experiences. Unfortunately for me, I had neither the confidence or swagger of a Daniel Craig, Richard Gere, or Brad Pitt. The extent of my cultural persona was a mosaic I constructed using their characters from *Casino Royale, Pretty Woman,* and *Meet Joe Black.* This of course was one of my closely guarded secrets.

I spent most of my childhood outside running, walking, or hiking. Nature's beauty, both perfect and imperfect, as well as its peace are what inspired me most. I'm far more adept at eating with my hands than at carefully maneuvering the knife and fork with the precision of a trained neurosurgeon.

So, I quickly checked myself when I realized amid the din of Lana's company party that I was shoveling appetizers. Little did I know back then (a year and a half already?) that Lana was focused on something else. If there was one thing I had going for me, it was authenticity. Lana's colleagues were un-original. They all looked and sounded the same, like a boring Baskin Robbins. Thinking back to that evening, I had no intention of standing out. I arrived at the gala in a light gray sport coat with navy pants, only to encounter a sea of black suits each carefully tailored.

"Lana, you didn't tell me this was a black-tie event."

"Matty, believe me, it's not. This is what everyone always wears."

"Should I have dressed more formally?" I asked. "People are going to mistake me for the valet."

"Don't be silly Matty. You look great."

"I'm just saying that if I am mistaken for a valet, I may decide to take one of your colleagues' expensive sports cars for a spin. I've always wanted to drive a Porsche and I can only imagine that there may be few in the parking lot."

Lana laughed, and we continued our banter until someone approached us and began speaking to her. Their conversation quickly devolved into a legalese topic which left me completely lost. My eyes drifted across the spacious Georgian Terrace ballroom. This was by far the fanciest and most ornate room I had ever been in. A large chandelier with crystal glass hung in the center of the room, illuminating the expansive parallel columns that reached two stories high. The second-story balconies complimented the ornate white crown molding, which appeared to be handcrafted. In the distance, tall windows with long white lace drapes were opened to the city, providing a soft breeze that swept through the room.

I overheard a conversation between two men who were complimenting one another on their Brioni and Saint Laurent suits, two brands which I had never heard of before. I took notice of all the people wearing cufflinks with their initials. When it comes to formal attire, I have an internal expiration clock, much like Cinderella and her glass slippers—after three hours I need to shed the formal attire for jeans and a t-shirt, or I become very grumpy and uncomfortable.

It was right at my expiration that the party evolved into a giant lovefest. Not even at my grandparent's fiftieth wedding anniversary, where all the friends and family members showered my doting grandparents with toasts, was the love flowing so freely. Lana and I stepped outside for a breath of fresh air.

"This is quite the party. Are all your company events like this?"

"No," answered Lana. "Not as long as I have worked here. No other company event even comes close to this. You have to realize though, our firm recorded record profits, which resulted in sizable bonus checks for everyone."

"Okay, that makes sense. My company's holiday parties are quite different."

"How so?"

"Well, many of the writers are introverts, which turns the level of partying down a notch for us. Also, I imagine our pay scales are dissimilar as well."

"So, your colleagues do not enter into endless comparisons of their *toys*?"

"What do you mean toys?"

"Matty, I literally just participated in a conversation where three men were attempting to one-up each other as they boasted about who has the fastest sports car."

"Well, I cannot say that I have ever compared my Prius to my boss's Camry. Unless an athlete or high-profile executive is visiting on a specific day, there is a low probability of seeing a Tesla in our parking lot."

"You're not like your peers though. I never heard you talk about yourself, much less about a material possession like your car or condo. Although, I am happy to hear that your co-workers have a strong kinship toward saving the environment. I greatly respect their passion toward being more environmentally aware."

"I guess there is one thread of commonality between you and my colleagues."

"To be honest, I am happy that the people in your firm excel at utilizing the Pareto principle, too."

Lana stopped. "What do you mean?"

"The Pareto principle more commonly known as the 80/20 rule. You see, as an introvert, I appreciate how the people you work with spend twenty percent of their time listening and eighty percent speaking. This has made the evening much easier for me. I can simply nod and ask a follow-up question, which minimizes the amount of energy I need to exert. Although, I must tell you, I cannot stay too much longer before my formal attire timeline expires."

Lana giggled. "Give me thirty more minutes and then I promise you can trade your tie for a t-shirt, and I'm more than happy to help you with that."

Lana disappeared for a short while to work the room while I passed the time listening in on other people's conversations. I became intrigued hearing the opinions and passions of Lana's co-workers, Raj and Kim. Raj went to great lengths educating Kim on the difference between buying a zero-emissions battery electric vehicle like his Tesla to the plug-in hybrid Porsche Cayenne she was considering. I remained silent listening to Raj. He spoke like a Tesla marketing executive and continued to pitch Tesla. Only at Kim's urging did I share the type of car I drove. Neither Raj nor Kim seemed particularly impressed with my Prius as the conversational tide shifted to taxes. I knew far less about taxes than cars. Turbo Tax provided me with the yearly paint by numbers approach to meeting the annual April 15 deadline. With essentially nothing to itemize and no investment beyond my 401K, taxes were a breeze for me. The depth of discussion between Raj and Kim was incomprehensible to me.

Then they started discussing celebrity role models. I estimated both Raj and Kim to be in their mid-fifties, which led to an interesting three-way dialogue. Their athletic role models were Chris Evert, Reggie Jackson, Muhammad Ali, and Kareem

Abdul-Jabbar, while mine were with Michael Jordan, Bo Jackson, and Ken Griffey Jr.

For the first time all evening, I felt comfortable speaking about a subject which I knew well. The three of us agreed that the athletes we looked up to were drastically different from today's athletes. We loved watching these sports figures compete at the highest level. Our generations bought their shoes, consumed what they consumed. Today, social media has provided a platform for the famous to share their personal beliefs openly and freely. Good or bad, we agreed that far fewer famous athletes stepped into controversy back then, because for the most part their personal lives remained private. Hypocrisy seemed much less prevalent, too.

Lana had joined the three of us when Raj looked directly at me and inquired how I felt about Fred Rogers.

The question seemed so random that I asked him to clarify. "Raj, are you asking me what I think about Fred Rogers more commonly known as Mr. Rogers?"

He grinned replying, "Yes, that's right."

I paused for a few moments, allowing me enough time to collect my thoughts. At this point in the evening, I'd had more than a few Stellas.

"You probably are unaware of this, but I grew up in Pittsburgh, where *Mr. Rogers' Neighborhood* was filmed. As a kid, *Mr. Rogers' Neighborhood* was my favorite show, and my mother would be the first person to share that when the show ended, I would start crying because I knew I had to wait twenty-four hours to watch *Mr. Roger's Neighborhood* again."

"So, he probably shaped your thinking and personality then?" asked Kim.

These were Lana's co-workers, so I wanted to be respectful. Still, I was confused about the Mr. Rogers stuff.

"I suppose I discovered the basics on understanding what feelings are and beyond that how to be kind, thoughtful, and compassionate."

"I can see those characteristics in you, Matty," said Raj with a smile.

"Thanks, Raj."

The conversation flow moved back towards business and a three-way discussion between Raj, Kim, and Lana. I kept thinking back to the line of questioning around Fred Rogers while my eyes looked across the vastness of the ballroom. Then I started to think and wonder about who the Fred Rogers of the current generation is, teaching the children basic principles. It seemed to me that Mr. Rogers has been displaced with smartphones. A video game application had become the modern-day substitute for Sesame Street. Kids with their eyes attached to an iPhone or iPad. There were no such distractions when I was a child. Generation X kids simply suffered until their parents were finished with whatever errand or event you were taken to.

When Lana finished her conversation with Raj and Kim, we walked to our room at the Renaissance Hotel about five blocks away, holding hands along Peachtree Street. The Fox Theater's green neon lights called attention to the night's headliner, Jason Mraz.

"Thank you Matty for coming with me tonight. It meant a lot to me that you were there to support me, and I know these types of parties are not exactly your preferred cup of tea."

I laughed. "Yes, I'm more of a coffee man, as you know."

"Do you know who you were talking to at the end of the night?"

Puzzled, I replied, "Yes, Raj and Kim. Why?"

"Yes, I know you know their names, but do you know who they are?"

"I just assumed they are co-workers of yours. Neither one of them provided any detail on what their roles were in your firm, if that is what you are asking. I just happened to be standing adjacent to them when the gravitational pull of conversation drew me in."

"Matty, those are the two partners of the firm. Raj and Kim own and run the entity. They must not have shared their last names, otherwise you would have known who they were."

Chuckling, I replied, "No, they were simply Raj and Kim to me. I had absolutely no idea who they were or what they did. Although, I was puzzled about the context of the Mr. Rogers questions."

"Don't worry about that Matty. They probably just had a little too much to drink."

"I figured so."

As I reflected on that fall evening at the Georgian Terrace a few years ago, I arrived at the realization of what attracted Lana to me. Her interest in me was a result of who I am and nothing more. Over the course of our relationship, Lana and I never discussed our salaries. We never had to. Clearly, Lana earns significantly more money than I do. It was refreshing for me to know that Lana loved me for the type of person I am and not what I do or how much I earn. Her affection toward me allowed me to be myself without any pretense.

Of course, all that mattered to me now was that the woman I was engaged to had been charged with a felony.

DINNER WITH THE ROMEROS

I took a shower after my run and anxiously waited for Eddie to return so that we could make dinner plans. I had just started reading a new book, *Make Your Bed: Little Things That Can Change Your Life . . . And Maybe the World,* when I heard muffled voices in the hall. Along with dialogue, there was the sound of the deadbolt being unlocked. When the door swung open, Honey raced to greet Eddie and his guest. I turned the corner and there he was, just as Eddie had described him. I felt like I had just exited the DeLorean ahead thirty years. Standing in front of me was the sixty-five-year-old version of Eddie. A grey-haired middle-aged Filipino with a strong jawline and comforting smile.

"Let me guess, you must be Mr. Romero?"

He grabbed my arm and pulled me in for a large bear hug.

"Absolutely, but please call me Menard."

Mr. Romero released me from his warm embrace, then bent toward Honey. "What a beautiful beast. Here kitty kitty."

Eddie looked puzzled. "Dad, she's not a cat, that is a dog."

"Oh, my mistake. I thought this was a lion."

"Who do you know that has a lion as a pet?"

"Mike Tyson. I learned that from the movie, *The Hangover*."

"But, in the movie, he has a pet tiger not a lion."

"What's the difference?" answered Mr. Romero.

I watched this father-son debate in amazement.

"I'm just kidding," said Mr. Romero finally. "I knew that it was a dog. You know she does look like a lion though. I think you boys could have some fun on Halloween."

"How so?" asked Eddie.

"You could dress her up more and take her trick-or-treating."

A large belly laugh followed. I assumed he knew that we were a bit too old to go trick-or-treating. What a character. I never met anyone with an energy level like his.

My phone started to ring. I bolted for the bedroom, hoping for Honey's sake that she would follow me. She didn't. Lana and I spoke for less than five minutes. Her lawyers were going to spend the better part of Friday night reviewing the case with her, so she urged me to have dinner with Eddie, and said that she would meet me for breakfast in the morning.

Eddie decided that we should have dinner at Blue Moon Pizza, which was not completely unexpected since we frequent the place regularly. What surprised me was that he was going to take his dad into the very establishment where the waitress he had his sights on worked.

The three of us walked along Pharr Road, then north on Peachtree toward Blue Moon Pizza. This was going to be interesting to say the least. The idea of Eddie and his father interacting with Eddie's crush was a nice diversion from the anxious thoughts that consumed me concerning Lana's felony charge.

Normally, Eddie was a complete extrovert. Until he came into proximity of Daisy. She was the one person that could render him speechless. Other than knowing her name and that she has butterfly tattoos on both wrists, we knew nothing about her. He was simply drawn to her physical beauty and friendly demeanor.

This was one of those beautiful fall nights that most northern transplants in Atlanta looked forward to after an endless, hot, humid, and sticky southern summer. Moving to Atlanta from Pittsburgh had been a major transition. I quickly fell in love with the early Spring and Summer, but soon came to loathe the month of August where the temperatures are approaching 90°F and the humidity peaks at about 75%. Within a few minutes of standing outside, I found myself covered in sweat. To compensate for the temperature and humidity, every building or home seems to run their air conditioning at artic levels. The transition from arctic cool to tropical breeze is a regular occurrence during the months of July and August. There's nothing like the fall once the August temperatures fade and the cool down starts in September.

When we arrived at the gray washed-brick building, Eddie thrust open the door as though he were Achilles stepping onto the battlefield. Three girls giggled when he winked at them. He took great pleasure in his cinematic entrances, which were somehow charming. Ever since I have known him, he's worked on making each entrance more dramatic than the previous one. A bold approach, given his less-than-intimidating stature. With neatly combed jet-black hair and a lean build, he stood less than six feet tall, so he was not threatening in the least. Curiously, I looked over at Mr. Romero to see what he thought of his son's grand gesture. He grinned happily while standing with his arms crossed behind his back.

Aside from throwing open the doors, the decibel level at which Eddie's voice projects creates a resonating buzz that could probably wake the dead were he to walk through a cemetery. Mr. Romero had a similar speaking style as he exclaimed, "Hey boys, the fire is grilling."

I had no idea what he meant. "Does that mean that the food smells good here?"

"No, you know the fire, the ladies are percolating," explained Mr. Romero.

Eddie added, "Yes Dad, they are percolating like a pot of coffee. There's a fine brew if you look over your left shoulder, but wait a few minutes before you do, because it will be too obvious to them if you turn around immediately."

Without hesitation, Mr. Romero turned his head. Three girls, two blonds and one brunette, playfully smiled at us, as it was obvious to them that we were not only talking about them but now gawking at them. He rotated his head back around, looking at us the way a puppy dog looks at someone offering them a milk bone. The happily married man was elated to be out on the town with his thirty-something son and his son's friend.

Scolding him, Eddie replied, "I told you not to turn around so quickly."

The three of us waited to be seated when my thoughts quickly drifted back to Lana. I was born a worrier, so anytime unexpected events occurred, I conjured up a vast range of potential outcomes and then worked through all the various scenarios that could occur. In this instance, I worried that my fiancée could be convicted and without knowing the legal implications, this frightened me. Lana was the consummate professional, so there had to be a rational explanation for this. She was the most ethical person I knew, so there was no way that she would partake in some insider trading operation. Beyond her principled ethics, Lana never strayed from the truth. There was no fathomable way she would partake in a despicable act such as insider trading. Eddie yanked me out of my fog as we were now ready to be seated.

The Blue Moon Pizza hostess complied with Eddie's request to be seated in Daisy's section. We sat at a small square table near the window, which provided an outside view of East Paces Ferry Road. Eddie and his father were engaged in a political conversation. My mind drifted from Lana to sports. Politics reminds me of the New York Yankees—a rich person's sport, like the Yankees payroll, the politicians like the high salaried Yankee players. To me the constituents were more like the Pittsburgh Pirates. These days politics has become the topic du jour, with everyday Americans rattling off the talking points created by the Washington, D.C., political consultants. The upcoming 2020 election only added fuel to the already divisive fire that was spreading throughout the country.

Eddie's dark green eyes exploded with excitement, and for the first time, his brain cooperated with his heart as he was able to speak clearly and freely. He smiled at Daisy, a smile she returned. At this point, Mr. Romero was also grinning as both he and Eddie looked up at the slender tall auburn-haired girl with long pigtails.

"Hi y'all, you're back again, can I get you anything to drink?"

Daisy disappeared after we ordered a pitcher of beer. The moment reminded me of a scene in *Field of Dreams* as Eddie's eyes followed Daisy, but instead of vanishing off into a corn field, she was out of sight behind the bar.

"Are you ok?" I asked.

"I think I'm in love," he answered.

"Yes, for me it will be love at first bite," added Mr. Romero.

Eddie paused as he shot a scolding glance his father's way. "There's something special about her, Matty. I can just feel it."

Even though we had only seen her once before and sat in her section, Daisy looked vaguely familiar to me, as though I had seen or met her before. As the night wore on, Daisy joined us at our table. I started to realize that Daisy and I were in some of the same journalism courses at UGA. I never knew or met her during my time in Athens, but I recognized her face.

It was the end of her shift, so Daisy started to tell us her life story as she sat down and made herself comfortable. She grew up in Cobb County and played soccer at Walton. Ironically, she knew Lana and had competed against her multiple times throughout high school. She must have been an elite player, because UGA offered her a soccer scholarship. Tragically, her career was cut short after she tore her ACL in her sophomore year.

Fast forward ten years later. Daisy now worked as a waitress and as an au pair. After an hour it was abundantly clear that Daisy was a dreamer, an idealist who was still struggling to find her way in the world. She made it sound like her goal of writing for the New York Times was insurmountable. The way she explained her life and experiences was disheartening, as though there was no hope or future for her to achieve her dreams and ambitions. She tried for the better part of the decade to land a job at a respectable newspaper or magazine, but to no avail. Her desire was to write about the impact of poverty on children. None of us had the courage to ask why she was so passionate about the topic. One topic of conversation faded into the next.

Despite the extreme differences in their careers and life paths, Eddie was deeply drawn to Daisy. He was hanging on to her every word. The two of them could not be more different. Eddie was a corporate lawyer who believed in unbridled capitalism. He knew that he always wanted to practice law and methodically pursued the career upon completing high school. Eddie avoided talking about himself, instead spending the time getting to know Daisy. I was interested to see how Eddie would navigate the intersection of corporate law and children born into poverty.

I marveled at how two vastly different people could get along so well. There was a romantic elegance to the entire conversation. If the entire country could communicate like this without inserting political talking points, the world would be a much better place.

As a once-aspiring novelist myself, I thought about what a great story I could start penning by writing about Eddie and

Daisy's budding romance. A first-generation Filipino lawyer who attains the American dream then falls in love with an aspiring writer and poverty activist trying to find her way in the world. Their relationship would be the perfect union. I imagined the two of them coming together to have the most fascinating dinner debates around socioeconomics. Their story would be an American story of yesteryear where people could disagree on a range of subjects but still have love and respect for one another. The idealist in me hoped so.

I could see that Mr. Romero was growing restless with all this serious conversation. "Excuse me miss," he asked. "What's a grape air?"

"Au pair, you mean, not grape air," she corrected.

"Yes, like you said, grape air."

"An au pair is a nanny who watches young children and is given a room to stay in the family's home in addition to her pay."

Mr. Romero unleashed a Fran Drescher-like laugh. "You're like Fran Drescher then from the Nanny?"

"Sure," replied Daisy, somewhat embarrassed.

It looked as though Eddie was about to spontaneously combust. His face turned firetruck red. Miraculously, he managed to divert the conversation back to Daisy's passion for writing. Her icy blue eyes sparkled after Eddie asked if she would be willing to share some of the pages she had composed.

Her energy level and excitement seemed to indicate that her lifelong dream was to be a great novelist, rather than a writer for the Times. The waitress and nanny gigs were just providing her with money to pay the bills. I too hoped Daisy provided Eddie with some of her work, since I was curious to read what she had written. Maybe her writing could be an inspiration to me?

When I was in college, I dreamed of penning my generation's *The Catcher in the Rye*. Until hearing this conversation, I had not thought about my dream in over a decade. It's sad when dreams evaporate into thin air almost like they never existed. Once I started working for the *New Atlanta Times*, the years flew by. Then I met Lana. I'd never given a second thought about writing a novel. I suppose because I write as a profession, the idea of writing for recreation lacked the appeal to pursue that old passion of mine.

I glanced down at my watch then stood up, excusing myself from the dinner party. I removed a twenty from my wallet, but Mr. Romero insisted that he pay for dinner. After thanking him and saying goodbye to everyone, I politely excused myself.

After all the events of the day, I needed some alone time. I often used the excuse that Honey needed to be let outside. It was true to some extent, but the introvert in me always relies on having the "dog at home" excuse as a way of escaping. I rather enjoy the company of others, but I'm one of those people with a social threshold. Lana can go hours upon end socializing, but I'm completely drained after about three or four hours of social activity. Tonight was particularly difficult.

I retrieved my phone from the left pocket of my jeans and dialed Lana. The call proceeded directly to her voicemail. I guess she was still in meetings with her lawyers. I left a short voice message letting her know that I was thinking about her, and I looked forward to seeing her for breakfast in the morning. Honey was elated when I returned. I too was happy to see a friendly face. We took an extra-long walk, taking in the beautiful autumn evening. The walk helped alleviate some of the stress of the uncertainty that I was facing.

The soft September breeze swept across my face. Honey wagged her tail as we shifted from a slow walk to a brisk trot. I had no intention of going for an evening jog, but the weather transported the two of us into our preferred environment. Honey started pulling me as she was fully expecting to run at our normal pace. Despite wearing blue jeans and Converse shoes, I complied, and we ended up putting in about five miles.

Eddie and his father still had not returned to the condo by the time Honey and I arrived. We were both exhausted after a long day and not one but two runs. I hoped to hit the sack and wake up to learn that everything concerning Lana's insider trading charge was just a bad dream.

SLEEPLESS NIGHT

I could not have registered more than three hours of sleep. I spent the night tossing and turning. Every time I have something pressing on my conscience, sleeplessness ensues. I've attempted to listen to music or to read, but no matter what I do to remedy the situation, I can never empty the endless stream of thoughts that traverse my mind.

The aspect of the entire insider trading saga that befuddled me the most was that Jack was somehow involved. I'd come to know Jack over time. We met on several different occasions at functions for Lana's firm. From what I understand, the yearlong relationship between Lana and Jack ended because of his presumptuousness. To say that Jack was self-involved would be greatly understating the truth.

Jack Reid came from old money. Within the span of the first five-minute conversation with him, I discovered how completely obvious his wealthy upbringing was. He provided me with a history lesson on how Buckhead was founded and how his family was personal friends with the founder. According to Jack, his great-great-great grandfather, or great to some nth degree, was personal friends with Henry Irby. In 1838, Henry Irby purchased 200 acres for $650 and subsequently named the town Irbyville. The name was eventually changed to Buckhead after Irby killed a large buck and mounted the deer's head in a noticeable location. As Jack narrated his long story, I became more curious about whatever happened to the mounted deer that Henry Irby killed. Everybody knows about Rudolph among the most famous of deer types; but how many people know about the deer that subsequently created the town name Buckhead? Hesitating for a second, I contemplated asking Jack if Mr. Irby named that buck. I restrained myself, but still the curiosity was killing me.

Jack found no humor when I quipped that he was raised in Irbyville. Irbyville always seemed to lack the prestige of the name Buckhead. To paraphrase Shakespeare, "What's in a name? That which we call a rose by any name would smell as sweet." I guess the name was important to Jack, because he went on to inform me that Buckhead is referred to as the Beverly Hills of the East. Who knew? I would have thought some section of Manhattan had more of a claim to the title. For the second time, I restrained myself, as much as I wanted to share my idea for a reboot of the *Beverly Hillbillies*, *Buckhead Hillbillies*. I didn't go there.

I came to learn that Jack's family founded a bank in Buckhead in the late 1800s. Jack's father lived on West Paces

Ferry Road on the same land that their family has owned since the founding of the town.

Jack was educated at Pace Academy, a private school in Atlanta. He graduated at the top of his class before enrolling at Duke University. From there, he went on to graduate magna cum laude from the law school at the University of Virginia. Before I could compliment him on his academic accolades, he made sure to tell me that he was accepted at both Yale and Harvard but didn't want to attend a liberal Yankee law school.

That first meeting with Jack, Lana stepped in to rescue me, as she puts it. "Don't say a word."

"Did you know that Buckhead was once called Irbyville, and that now really rich people live here?" I asked her.

I could see now how someone like Jack would be involved in a slimy scheme with one of his investment banking buddies where they exchanged inside information to profit from a stock trade. It would be just like Jack to exchange confidential information with one of his Duke investment banking buddies.

What a guy, I thought now, as I looked over at Honey while making my way to the bathroom. As I lifted my toothbrush, I caught a glimpse of myself in the mirror. I felt like the grim reaper must be nearby. It looked like death was falling upon me. I set my toothbrush down and splashed cold water onto my face, hoping to erase the sleepiness from my eyes.

Lana would meet me for breakfast soon. How would that conversation go? I was still trying to piece together why or how Lana could be involved. Our wedding was less than a year away. She wanted a dream wedding. Despite her father's willingness to contribute, the two of us were paying for the wedding ourselves. Lana was shouldering most of the financial burden. Could she be skimming money from the company to help her pay for the wedding? No, that can't be it.

What is it?

BREAKFAST

Lana and I planned to meet in the lobby of the Eclipse. I was sitting across from the elevators when the elevators opened to the soft tone of Lana's voice. She appeared with her friend, Irene, who was taking Lilly the beagle for a walk. Lilly and Honey were good friends, so Lilly was happy to see me. She sniffed me for a minute or two until she realized that Honey wasn't around. I petted the tri-colored beagle until Lilly pointed her nose to the ground pulling Irene towards the door.

"Bye, Matty. Nice seeing you," said Irene.

Lana looked as beautiful as she always did, without any indication of worry or stress. I seemed to be suffering more from her circumstances than she was. She extended her arm to pull me up from the bench. I pulled her close to me like I was hugging an old friend I hadn't seen in years. Lana grabbed me by the hand and led me outside. I guess she made the unilateral decision that we would be walking to the Buckhead Bread Company for breakfast.

We started east on Pharr Road for the mile-long walk. I liked the prospect of walking and it beat trying to compete for a parking spot at the popular breakfast destination. I was cautious about asking too many questions about her insider trading charge. I had no idea what she was feeling or how to broach what could be a very delicate subject. Lana started off with casual conversation by inquiring, "How was dinner with Eddie?"

"You mean the Romeros. Eddie's dad was there too."

"Really?"

"Yep. Mr. Romero is quite the character. Imagine Eddie twenty-five years from now with gray hair. They both talk at the same decibel level too."

"Where did you guys go?"

"We went to Blue Moon for pizza and of course we had to sit in Daisy's section."

"Eddie's still chasing after her then?"

I shrugged. "That's one he cannot let go."

"Good for him. I hope things work out for Eddie and Daisy."

"You never mentioned that you and Daisy were soccer rivals."

"Yes, I know. It was so long ago. I didn't even think she would remember me. We really didn't know each other except for playing against each other a few times a year."

We waited for about fifteen minutes before we were seated at a small two-person table near the window looking out to Piedmont Road. I had so many questions that I wanted to ask, but I didn't want to be the one to bring up the topic. Breakfast was served and consumed and up to that point Lana never broached the topic of her new legal troubles.

She must have sensed my tension. Lana put down her coffee mug, took my hand, and then looked into my eyes. I tried to look away, but I was drawn into her dark chocolate eyes.

I believed Lana was my soulmate but hated when she or anyone looked deep into my eyes. Every time someone attempted to make eye contact with me, it felt as though they were staring right into my soul. I realize that it's unreasonable to think that someone or anyone can determine your innermost thoughts and feelings by looking into your eyes, but hey.

Lana told me that everything would work out for the best— told me that she was looking out for my best interest by not getting me involved. She promised to share as much as she could but stressed the less that I knew the better, if I were to be subpoenaed.

She said that when we were alone, she would share more details of the charges. She apologized for not being more forthright at breakfast, explaining that there were too many people present at the restaurant to have the type of conversation that I so wanted to have. I wondered why Lana would suggest going to a public place in the first place. Without sharing anything confidential or that would implicate me, Lana deciphered the context of what was published in the *Atlanta Journal Constitution* about the situation.

Basically, both Jack and she were being charged with advising a third party of several mergers that they were underwriting. The third party took the information that only their firm and clients knew about and traded stocks with the secret information. I knew this was all Jack's doing. It seemed to follow my original hypothesis. Jack and his rich buddies were trying to make a quick buck using inside information.

"Is one of Jack's friends involved in this?" I asked.

"Matty, this isn't the time or place to talk about any details."

Lana would not share any names of the third party or indicate whether I knew the person. She stressed again and again that she was completely innocent. The truth would come out as the trial unfolded. For the first time since the news broke, I believed Lana and was confident that she was not involved. I could sense something different, though. The experience she had was impacting her in ways which she wasn't letting on.

Lana and I went our separate ways after breakfast. Lana usually spent Saturday afternoon working. I returned to the Eclipse to pick up Honey and the two of us piled into the Prius and drove north to Dahlonega. The fall leaves were exploding with color, and the warm delicate breeze was refreshing as we walked along the Appalachian from Amicalola Falls toward Springer Mountain. For a moment, albeit a noticeably short one, I considered the possibility of continuing straight through to Maine.

Reality set in minutes later as I contemplated not only our lack of gear, which included a few protein bars and a liter of water, but also my companion. I loved Honey more than anything, but hiking with her was no small task. Every time a squirrel or rabbit appeared, she darted off, nearly yanking my shoulder out of its socket.

I removed Honey's water dish and filled it with water. I sat on a nice flat rock covered with thick lush moss. A young couple, who I assume were in high school based on their Milton Eagle sweatshirts, stopped for a moment to pet Honey. The couple reminded me of Lana. I wished that she had come with us on this beautiful fall day instead of spending the afternoon toiling away in her home office.

Lana was the love of my life, and I could not fathom what my life would be like without her. I'd never met or dated anyone like her before. She possessed a beauty that I had never experienced prior. She had a pure heart and kindness like no other. I had trouble envisioning her as a lawyer, especially after meeting some of her colleagues. She was nothing like them. I imagined her more as an immigration attorney with her sympathetic nature.

I struggled with the fact that she was being charged with illegal activity of any kind, let alone insider trading. It wasn't like Lana to seek after material gains. She grew up in an upper-middle class family where her father was a chemical engineer, her mother a physical therapist. Both she and her older brother paid their way through Georgia Tech. As well dressed and well off as she might now be, she was hardly shopping at Celine or Hermes. She had no debt except for her mortgage. A wedding coming up, sure, but that wouldn't be too over the top. What would be her motive for risking her freedom and career?

There was absolutely no difficulty for me to conceive that Jack would be involved in some sleazy scheme to make a quick buck. The only thing he ever talked about was money, or all things pertaining to money. That Jack . . . I spent a little time wondering about that Jack on my way back home with Honey.

INSIDER TRADING

On the drive back to Buckhead from Dahlonega, I decided to do some research.

I arrived back to the Eclipse shortly after six and showered before heading up to Lana's condo for dinner. She was in the middle of preparing dinner for the two of us and didn't expect me until 7. I attempted to hide my ulterior motive for arriving early by acting like I wanted to help her cook.

Lana was too smart for my little trick, knowing full well that I hated cooking.

"What is the real reason you showed up so early? And I don't want to hear that you wanted to help me or that you just wanted to spend more time with me. I know you too well, and that look of curiosity on your face is a dead giveaway that you are up to something."

There was no fooling her. "Honestly, I wanted to do some reading about insider trading. Can I borrow one of your law books to read up on the subject?"

"You can't be serious. You of all people, you despise lawyers and now you want to dive right into the legalities of mergers and acquisitions?"

I prodded Lana and after ten minutes of pleading, she selected a textbook from the middle of her bookshelf.

For the next forty minutes, I painstakingly navigated my way through American insider trading laws and regulations. I think in doing so I had discovered the solution to my sleepless nights. Who needs to count sheep when you can open a bedside text to read about SEC rules and regulations?

Honestly, I was skimming more than reading after a while as I flew through the topics of statutory law, SEC regulations, and court decisions. It all boiled down to a person having non-public information about a company and using that information to trade a public company stock.

It all seemed absurd on some level or another. Any high-level employee at any company in the world would have information that no one else would have access to and could conceivably share that data with any friend, relative, or colleague. It's not like those working for large companies treat their jobs like CIA operatives. How in the world could anyone police this stuff?

The entire system of trading stocks appeared to be rigged. As I continued to turn the pages of this utterly boring text, I concluded that the entire middle class is disadvantaged compared to those who work on Wall Street or K Street. For the first time in my life, I was finally able to link the capitalists and the politicians. It's no wonder some of the wealthiest people in the country come from these two groups. It stands to reason that those on Wall Street would have knowledge about companies that an average farmer in Nebraska wouldn't. Wall Street executives have access to the stock analysts who have access to the CEOs of these large companies. Likewise, the lobbyists and advocates in Washington, D.C., who have offices on K Street possess the very wisdom that will drive legislation that will provide an advantage to a specific company.

After Lana and I sat down to dinner, I started in on her a bit. "Listen, I know you can't talk about your case, but what strikes me about security fraud is that it would be nearly impossible for the SEC to monitor and enforce the sharing of proprietary information."

She smiled and placed her hand on mine. "Let me begin by saying that I think it's adorable that you love me so much that you are willing to spend your Saturday night studying insider trading statutes, but I don't want you to worry about this."

"Lana, how can I not be concerned about these allegations? You could end up in a federal prison for twenty years."

She gently stroked my hair and glanced into my eyes. "Will you wait for me if I get twenty years?"

"For you my love, I would wait a hundred years."

"Then please Matty, just be patient and I promise everything will work out."

I knew that at this point she wanted to discuss something else, but all this newly discovered subject matter was at the top of my mind.

"Ok, I won't talk about your case anymore, but it seems to me, one of the best ways to reduce this insider trading is to break the link between Wall Street and K Street."

Lana lifted her glass of red wine and took a sip. She nodded. "You're amazing. My fiancée the sportswriter has single-handedly discovered the solution to eliminating crony capitalism."

"It will never happen though."

"Why not?"

I shrugged. "There's too much money and power involved on both sides. All these politicians and investment bankers attended the same Ivy League schools, and although they pretend to despise each other, it's all theater. The bankers and politicians have all become millionaires or multi-millionaires because of the influence they have on gaming the system. There's no way a lifetime Congressman should be worth more than ten million dollars. There's no incentive for anyone to clean up this corruption because it's a zero-sum game, and if you get rid of the lobbyists and advocates, then they stand to lose money and so do the politicians.

Lana laughed. "For someone who distrusts politicians and lawyers, you seem to be deeply passionate about this subject. I enjoy seeing you so engaged, and I think if you really wanted, you could do something to address this corruption."

"How could I possibly resolve crony capitalism? You just put it best—I'm a local Atlanta sportswriter."

"No. You're much more than a beat writer for the *New Atlanta Times*. You're a brilliant writer who has always wanted to pen the next great American novel. Maybe this could be the subject of your book, and if it's a bestseller, it would reach millions of people."

Over the course of the evening, I searched for the best opportunity to seek what was really eating at Lana. I needed to arrive at the heart of the matter. I seized the opportunity when I noticed her sigh and drifting into a deep thought. "Lana, I know you fairly well, right?"

"Yes of course Matty. Why do you ask?"

"Because I can see that something happened that is tearing you apart. Please, tell me what it is."

Lana sighed. "I would rather not."

"Please Lana, I would like to know what is bothering you."

"Ok Matty, I'll tell you, but please do not ask me to discuss this again. The experience I had is one I would like to forget."

A fearfulness entered Lana's eyes as she began to tell me about her experience.

"The first thing I recall is being surrounded by a team of FBI agents dressed in navy blue windbreaker jackets with the yellow FBI inscription on the front and back. Two male agents took me by the arms, placing them behind my back while reading me my rights. I did not say a word. The next thing I knew I was placed in the back of one of their four-door black sedans and was driven to a holding cell. The next few hours felt like years while I sat in a small cell with two other women. The one woman was a drug addict and kept screaming in agony for help. The sound of her screams, ugh. The other woman had been arrested for shoplifting. She was a younger woman in her early twenties, and she was charged with stealing food from Whole Foods. My heart ached for both women who were suffering through difficult times in their lives. My situation could not be any more different than theirs. I did nothing wrong or illegal, and I have never had to overcome an addiction or worry about when or how to acquire my next meal. The judge informed me how fortunate I was to be released on the same day of my arrest. Most people are not so lucky. For as long as I live, I do not know if I will ever escape the pain I witnessed on those women's faces, or the agony that sprung forth from their words."

I reached across the table and placed my hand on top of Lana's. I said nothing. There were no words to comfort her or to relieve her of that unforgettable experience. I was happy that Lana shared with me what had her so troubled. In the past, she would not have done so. Lana would have concealed her thoughts and pain and worked through her feelings by herself.

Still, I struggled to see how the FBI could have confused Lana for being involved in a conspiracy like she was being accused of. Even as she described the horrible experience in the holding cell, it was strange to me that she could somehow even be linked to such a crime.

DYING BREED

With Honey in tow, we set out for a long run the next morning on the Roswell River Walk. The two of us can usually go an entire five miles without stopping for hydration, but I accounted for a longer run and harnessed a water pack around my torso. After about seven miles or so on the trail, I sensed Honey needed some water, so we stopped. She looked tired and hot, so we ran back toward the car. Honey loved running along the Chattahoochee River and all the sites and associated smells. There were plenty of birds and squirrels vying for her attention as we trotted along the banks of the river. My favorite part of the run was the boardwalk. It reminded me of spending summer vacations at Ocean City, Maryland, as a kid.

After our run, we drove to Crazy Love Coffeehouse. They are famous for their Belgian waffles, which Lana prefers. I typically opt for the avocado toast on sourdough with a cold nitro brew. Their avocado toast has the perfect combination of avocado, tomatoes, and cilantro. On more than one occasion, Lana has accused me of being a "wannabe millennial."

Whatever. It's delicious.

While Honey and I sat on the curb of Canton Street, a stranger approached me.

"Excuse me, but are you Matthew Brusco?" he inquired.

"Yes sir, have we met before? I apologize but I do not recognize you."

The tall and slender man with salt and pepper hair and black rimmed glasses answered, "No, we have never met, but I'm a huge fan of your columns."

Standing up, I extended my hand to shake his hand. "Thank you, sir. I really appreciate that."

"Well, keep up the good work."

With that, he walked by and entered the coffee shop. I am recognized only on the rarest of occasions, perhaps a few times a year. Older writers of my parents and grandparent's generation describe the fans of newspaper sports writers as a dying breed. The generations before mine were often recognized in public because they were the source of information where people acquired their information on sports.

Each time I am recognized as a local sportswriter, I am flattered. I almost feel that I have an obligation to provide the person with more than a simple thank you. I thought maybe I should have bought that gentleman a cup of coffee but at the same time, I am cognizant of respecting one's privacy. On more than one occasion, someone has asked what a day in the life of a beat writer is like. I can better explain a season in the life versus a day in the life. Major League Baseball beat writers' seasons begin in mid-February during spring training when rising new players compete for a roster spot to play in the big leagues and veterans fine tune their skills to be ready for opening day in April. The beautiful part of spring training for northern beat writers is the temporary escape of the winter weather to the warmer climates of Arizona or Florida. Aside from the nice weather, beat writers ease into the season beginning their day around 8 AM.

When opening day arrives in April, the marathon begins and runs until the playoffs begin in October. On a typical day, I arrive at the ballpark in the middle of the afternoon around 3 PM. I start preparing for a long day which will ultimately end by 11 PM if I'm lucky enough to beat my deadline. I start constructing my storyline around 3:30 when I visit the clubhouse to interview players. One of the greatest challenges of a writer is to maintain a thick skin while managing the ever-changing relationship dynamics of forty-plus people, which includes twenty-five players, managers, coaches, and scouts. Depending on the nature and tone of the last article, a player may love or hate me on any given day. That is the nature of the business, where maintaining objectivity is paramount to writing high quality work.

After participating in the daily press meeting with the manager, I join the other writers and reporters in the press box to have dinner before the first pitch. Creativity commences inning after inning as I take notes, keep statistics, score the game, and incorporate key elements I discovered from earlier conversations with the players or the Q&A session with the manager. After the game ends, I head back down to the clubhouse to obtain more quotes and comments for the game before finally returning to the press box to complete my article and send it to print before my deadline. Then I leave the stadium by 11 PM if I am lucky enough and drive home ten miles from Truist Park to Buckhead. This is the life when the Braves play in Atlanta.

The functional part of my job remains the same on the road with the main difference being the one hundred and twenty or so nights spent in hotel rooms and the early morning flights. The last night of a three-game series on the road constitutes getting to bed at 1 AM and waking up three and half hours later to fly to the next destination. Over time, I acquired the ability to fall asleep on the plane before the flight attendant closed the boarding door. Friends and strangers share their feelings of how great they perceive my job to be. I too recognize how fortunate I am to have stumbled into the occupation of dreams. What does not fully resonate for those who have not traveled for business is the lifestyle is far less alluring than anyone would perceive it to be.

People take for granted having the opportunity to return from the office every day to one's home. Only on the rarest of occasions do I get the taste of a home cooked meal. There's also the comfort of sleeping in a bed of your own as opposed to the hotel bed du jour provided by whatever Marriott chain has been booked. Without a wife and kids, I have no responsibility to return home to be a husband or father, but that would be a challenge in my current profession. Many people in my profession do this, but I know from what has been shared with me the strain and toll traveling places on their relationships. I get other ancillary benefits like status with the airlines, hotels, and rental car companies, which provide me with opportunities to further travel to places that I otherwise could not afford. Would I trade my job for another? No way. Not under present circumstances. Would I consider something different with Lana and a future family in the picture? Absolutely.

I hope to continue to do what I love for as long as I possibly can. There are countless others that would trade places with me in a heartbeat. Writing for the Braves allows me to derive the nostalgic feel of living life at a slower pace that I craved since I was a child. Often, I imagine an era when people took the time to parse page by page through printed news. My grandfather spent hours a day reading multiple local Pittsburgh papers. He went section by section, always spending the most time on the sports pages. There were two house rules when "borrowing" his newspaper. First, do not crinkle the pages. The paper had to be folded neatly and not creased improperly. Second, the crossword puzzles were off limits. Completing those was the grand finale of finishing the daily papers for him.

My generation of writers had become unknowns to many of our readers. We were simply a name and there was little association of the picture that was placed at the top of the column alongside the title of the article. Readers require less information from sportswriters than in the previous decades. Back then, there was no social media, therefore a sportswriter was the go-between for information from the athletes and coaches to the public. Social media has changed the game for everyone. Now the athletes have direct access to their fans through Twitter, Facebook, or Instagram. They have the following instead of the writers because the information is direct and unfiltered.

I enjoy the modern-day style and the idea that there still is a need for a writer like me because the story of the game or series still needs to be told. Personally, I see social media as a win-win. My audience consists of readers, which are different from the viewers or listeners that broadcast journalists need to address. Writing allows me to tell the story as I see the world. My style of prose transports the reader to a different time and place.

I prefer to write about the game itself rather than any individual person because there still are many people who can only experience a sporting event through reading. I have always aspired to write in a way that allows the reader to put themselves in the stands. My aim is to share the details that cannot be seen through television. The smell of the fresh popcorn being sold by the vendors is never shared by a broadcaster sitting three stories up in a booth. Sure, the sounds of the ball meeting the wooden bat can be heard. But it's different.

What is often missed or rarely described to the viewing audience is the expressions on the faces of the pitcher and hitter. Everything happens so fast that people gravitate toward watching the ball and the trajectory of the ball after the hitter makes contact. A sportswriter that is seated close enough to the field can fixate on people. One of my favorite game day pleasures is watching a little leaguer get an autograph from their major league idol right before the game. Boys' and girls' eyes light up like fireworks on the Fourth of July when they are fortunate enough to hand their ball or glove to a professional ball player. They patiently wait as the athlete scribes their name on the article with a black Sharpie marker.

There's nothing like watching a parent teach their child how to keep score the old-fashioned way using a pencil and the program. This is the essence of baseball. The game itself has become a dying breed, which saddens me. People prefer the faster pace of football or basketball, but that is because we have lost the art of nuance. The idiosyncrasies that can only be learned at a major league ballpark. These traditions need to be passed down from generation to generation. The failure to do so is why baseball has lost its popularity. Instead of seeing engaged parents and their children watching and capturing every detail of the game, what one tends to find is the parent and child with their faces buried into their respective smart devices.

The magic of the game has disappeared.

Still, I am the luckiest guy in the world because, at least for the time being, I get to be the seven-year-old boy who learned the traditions of baseball from his grandfather. I have never shared that with anyone. From the first time my grandfather took me to the ballpark as a kid, I knew I wanted to be part of the game. I craved the sights, sounds, and smells of the ballpark and to this day, I still do. I knew that I would never be good enough to play professionally. One way or another, I discovered a profession which provided me with a way to live out my dreams. Today, I get paid to write about the experiences I loved for over thirty-some years. I may be a dying breed, but I am proud to be one, nonetheless.

Wow, I thought as I sat there in front of the coffee shop. *Look what a good run and a friendly face can do.*

CLASH OF THE TITANS

The next several weeks passed by quickly and before I knew it, October was over. With each passing day, normalcy returned as I thought less and less about Lana's trial. We were spending most of our time preparing for our September 2020 wedding, which was now less than a year away. I was walking Honey on a cool Wednesday evening when I received a text from my cousin Mike.

Mike lived in northern California where he worked as an investment banker. His text said that he would be arriving in Atlanta on Friday morning for a business meeting and asked if we could meet for dinner that night, to which I agreed.

I think the last time I saw Mike was at Christmas five years earlier in Pittsburgh. We were both back in town for the holidays and we met at my aunt and uncle's house for breakfast one morning. Mike and I were close as kids growing up, but distance and years had made it more difficult to stay in touch. He was several years older than I was, and I always looked up to him like a big brother.

My Friday plans with Mike proved once again that the problem with clichés is that, often, they're true. In this case, "it's a small world" came to mind when Mike and I ran into Jack—and not in a good way.

My life had finally started to return to normal, and then suddenly Jack emerged, bringing about thoughts of Lana and the trial. It was after Mike and I had finished eating dinner at the Highland Tap. We walked south along Highland Avenue to Hand in Hand. Hand in Hand was one of my favorite pubs in the Highlands, and we planned on having a beer there before calling it a night.

Lana was right to suggest that we take a taxi to dinner, because both Mike and I were in no condition to drive between having a few drinks at the Highland Tap then another couple at Hand in Hand. I was in the middle of a conversation with Mike when I felt this large hand come down and swat me on the back. I stumbled forward before turning around to see Jack standing in front of the two of us.

Mike extended his hand to Jack introducing himself. "Hello, I'm Mike Andrews, Matty's cousin."

Moments later I felt as though I was living out the Harvard bar scene in *Good Will Hunting* where the understated Will quickly psychoanalyzes the wealthy Harvard graduate student. In this case though, the role of Will was being played by my cousin, Mike Andrews. Unbeknownst to Jack was that underneath the tattered blue jeans, faded gray t-shirt, and unshaven face, Mike ran a phenomenally successful investment banking firm in the Bay area.

"Matty's cousin, huh. I insist on buying you a drink," said Jack.

Mike ordered a club soda which for some reason infuriated Jack. "Club soda? Why don't you order a man's drink, son?"

Mike shot me a quick glance trying to discern if this was my friend or merely some odd acquaintance. We made eye contact and Mike nodded. I soon recognized that Mike wasn't going to let it slide.

Both men stood about six feet even, but that's where the similarity between the two ended. Mike was lean and strong with a physique built by regular surfing and running. Jack on the other hand was husky with broad shoulders and a protruding belly. Honestly, I never thought for once that a physical altercation would ensue. First, both had too much to lose and really nothing to gain. If the two did come down to blows, I knew that my 150-pound frame wasn't going to get in the middle of it.

"Is there something wrong with club soda?" asked Mike.

"No, not at all. I guess it's some California thing where you are too good for a beer or cocktail. You probably only eat organic food as well, even though the organic food you pay extra for probably grows right across the street from the non-organic fertilized food and when the wind blows, your organic produce is not so organic anymore after it's covered with fertilizer."

Mike nodded as though he were accepting Jack's thoughts about him.

Jack continued.

"What is it you do in California?"

"I'm in finance," Mike answered.

"You probably work for a small start-up out there, don't you?"

"Something like that. Since we seem to be playing the guessing game, I'll bet you're a lawyer."

"Yep. Is it that obvious?"

"Well, first off, you're a smug ass and I'm accustomed to working with your sort. You're probably the prized product of a wealthy family and judging from that deep southern drawl, you came from old money, meaning you inherited most of what you have. You probably attended private schools your entire life and grew up with like-minded friends who came from the same socio-economic background as you. Then your daddy sent you to an expensive private university, after which he footed the bill for an overpriced law school. Then you graduated and he pulled a few strings by asking one of his golf buddies to hire you because your grades were less than spectacular, and you found yourself in the bottom third of your graduating class. Does that about sum it up?"

Jack's face turned fire-truck red, and it looked like he was going to take a swing at Mike, but then he recoiled his fist and lifted his beer bottle from the bar and vanished. Mike had just done what I always wanted to do, but never had the courage. Of course, Mike is bigger, stronger, and smarter than me too.

I spent the next hour updating Mike on the charges Lana was facing and Jack's involvement. It's moments like the exchange between Mike and Jack where you can identify the significant ones in your life among the insignificant others. A significant other always has your best interests in mind and protects you while insignificant others like Jack take cheap shots and try to break you down.

Mike left for California the next morning, but not before meeting Lana for the first time over breakfast. The three of us discussed the exchange with Jack the previous evening. Lana said she very much would have liked to see it, but at the same time she was glad that she wasn't there.

Lana and I had separate plans for Saturday evening. She planned to have dinner with her mom at the Georgian Terrace Hotel before attending the *Dirty Dancing* musical at the Fox. My longtime friend David and I were headed to Eddie's Attic in Decatur to see Kevin Griffin from Better than Ezra. David was a significant one in my life, and he has been ever since we graduated high school.

The history of our friendship traces back to Pittsburgh. We attended the same elementary school through third grade until the school district redistricted the geographic school boundaries. During elementary school we knew each other, but we really didn't become great friends until the night of our high school graduation. David is extraordinarily funny and a natural storyteller. I came to learn from David that he thought I was a rebellious kid in elementary school and his opinion of me continued into high school, including the time in ninth grade when I sported the early 1990s skateboard haircut: a side part with shaved hair on the sides and back.

I don't think I was ever too rebellious, and David can confirm that after knowing me as well as anyone from 1996 through today. Our friendship grew from our freshman year of college on through graduation and eventually David asked me to be in his wedding. The one constant that has always been part of our friendship is our appreciation for the band Better than Ezra (or "BTE," as we like to call them).

Girlfriends came and went but the one thing the two of us always clung to was BTE. I can place almost any time and event of my life to a given BTE song. David and I have seen BTE all over the east coast. It's difficult to count the road trips we took together to see them play. Some that immediately come to mind are Cleveland, Hershey, Philadelphia, Auburn, Jackson, Birmingham, and New Orleans.

One of the most memorable trips was in college, where David and I, along with my younger brother, Scott, and his younger sister, flew to Houston, Texas, on a Mardi Gras weekend. We had the best of intentions, planning to make the six-hour drive to New Orleans and see BTE at Tipitina's. After six long hours in a white Chevy Malibu rental car, we arrived in New Orleans and parked along Canal Street.

The four of us took in a Mardi Gras parade where we collected a new wardrobe of beads from the floats. After the parade we made our way over to French Quarter and observed the chaos of Bourbon Street. We then attempted to head back to the car and drive to Tipitina's. Some things just are not meant to be. Despite our best efforts, we struggled to even make it back to Canal Street with all the madness of the crowds and parades.

A local New Orleaner dissuaded us from attempting to drive from our parking space near the Superdome to Napoleon Avenue. With each passing minute reality set in and by midnight, I looked over at David and he gave me a nod. A nod from a good friend is all it takes to realize that it's time to go. With that the four of us packed up and headed back to Houston.

Neither David nor I thought about driving back to Houston in the wee hours of the morning. David, Scott, and Danielle all fell asleep and honestly, I have no idea how I managed to get back home. When the sunrise woke David, he quickly discovered that I was circling Houston's beltway. We found a gas station where we bought some cheap coffee-machine cappuccinos and within a few hours we were boarding a US Air flight back to Pittsburgh. That was fourteen years ago.

Today David is happily married and a dad, so I'm appreciative of any time I get to hang out with him. We arrived at the red brick building with a red neon Eddie's Attic sign. Neither one of us had been to Eddie's Attic before, but we were familiar with the history of the place where many artists launched their careers including John Mayer, Jennifer Nettles, and Shawn Mullins.

David and I had seats at a table about ten feet from the stage. Kevin nonchalantly made his way onto the stage carrying his acoustic guitar. As he started playing old songs, it felt as though we were going back in time and reliving past events of our life. Despite the brief trip down memory lane, things felt different. It was obvious that life was changing for all of us, Kevin included. That's the nature of aging and it's not necessarily a bad thing. I was as happy as I had ever been with my upcoming wedding to the love of my life.

After the show, David and I headed over to the Thinking Man Tavern on West Howard Avenue. We wanted to grab one last final beer before taking our respective Uber rides home. The two of us sat at the bar reminiscing about old times. We were talking about Lana and the insider trading and Jack's involvement when David said, "Matty, Jack is Lana's insignificant one."

"What do you mean, insignificant one?"

"You see, we all have an insignificant one or ones in our life. Sometimes the most consequential one is also the most insignificant."

"How do you mean we all have them?"

"At some point, someone enters our life and alters the path that we were proceeding along. Upon entering your life, the said person causes you to make a decision that leads to an outcome that is going to be different than if you had stayed on your current path."

"And how is Jack that person for Lana?"

"It does not have to be Jack, but just for sake of argument, let's say it's him. Was Lana involved with anyone before Jack?"

"Yes, why do you ask?"

"Who was it?"

"I think his name was Edgar. They dated during college until she met Jack."

David paused. "Ok Matty, I don't know this to be a fact but give me some latitude here. Let's assume the relationship between Edgar and Lana was good. Not great but good. The natural progression for college sweethearts would be to get engaged and married after college. Lana and Edgar may well have gotten married when they graduated from Georgia Tech. But something happened. Something always happens. Along comes Jack who for whatever reason causes Lana to rethink her relationship with Edgar and ultimately leads to her ending the relationship with him and then to start dating Jack. At the point they are dating, Jack becomes Lana's significant other. Things proceed for a while, a year maybe, and then the relationship dissolves, each going their separate way. Then you met Lana, right?"

"Yes," I answered. I was intrigued. "That's the sequence in which the events unfolded and when I met Lana. Why?"

"Jack is Lana's insignificant other. He caused her to end the relationship with Edgar and in doing so, he may have stopped Lana from marrying Edgar. In the end, you are now Lana's significant other, but if not for Jack, who played a significant role in Lana's life path causing her to alter courses, the two of you may not have ended up engaged. Lana could be married to Edgar. Sometimes the most insignificant people in our lives play the most significant roles."

"People enter and exit our lives. Some wind up changing our life trajectory."

"Yes, we all probably have an insignificant other or who knows, maybe a few. These are the people that over the long run will be long forgotten about. But if not for our life's intersection with them, our lives would be completely different than they otherwise are today."

"Would you mind if I borrowed 'Insignificant Others or Ones' for the title of a book?"

"Not at all. But you may want to check first on the originality of the titles. Are you ready to head out?"

With that, the two of us left the bar and headed home. Sitting in the back of the black Nissan Murano, I kept thinking back to David's explanation of how we come to arrive at life's destinations.

THE HOLIDAYS

By November, Lana and I were spending most of our time preparing for our wedding, which was now less than a year away. As always, my walks with Honey were a chance to step away and take a breath. On this particular Thanksgiving eve, I received a call from my mom.

I will never forget that day, November 13, 2014. Not only was this my grandfather's birthday, but my mother also tearfully informed me that his cancer was worsening and urged me to travel back to Pittsburgh to say goodbye. As my mother continued to speak, I could not make out a single word as my body and mind became numb.

"Matty, are you still there?" she tearfully asked.

I struggled to find the words. Just as I thought life was returning to normal again . . . boom. My grandfather and I were close. I was the oldest grandson, and I always had the feeling that he was my biggest fan. Regardless of whether it was athletics or academics, he was always there encouraging me.

Poppy, as we called him, was the person who inspired me to become a sportswriter. He never directly suggested that I should pursue journalism in college, but sports were such a large part of my childhood and my relationship with him that sportswriting seemed like the natural path to follow. He and I spent countless summer nights at his outdoor patio listening to Pirates games. Even though we were thirty or so miles from the stadium, he would curse at the players when they made an error or struck out. I almost had the feeling that he thought he was sitting in the dugout next to Jim Leyland and it was his responsibility to discipline the players.

My grandmother, or Nanny as we affectionately referred to her, would scold him for cursing around us. She could care less about "ball games" as she rocked on her five-foot-wide benched swinger that stood a way off from the brick patio where Poppy and I sat. There was a white metal wire table with four chairs, and he always sat in the chair closest to the sliding door that entered their finished basement. I cannot remember a time when he wasn't sipping a ten-ounce Iron City Beer while taking a drag from his Winston cigarette. In addition to hearing Steve Blass and Lanny Fraterre's voices over the radio, there was the constant sound of bugs getting zapped. My grandparents loved their neon bug zapper, which hung adjacent to the sliding door entering the house.

"Matty, are you still there?" asked my mom.

"Sorry, Mom. Yes, I'm here. I'll be on the first flight out tomorrow."

As soon as I returned to the condo, I called Lana to let her know that I wouldn't be attending Thanksgiving dinner with her and her family. She asked if she could come with me to be there for me, but I declined her offer. I was feeling numb and just wanted to be alone to navigate my sea of emotions. Lana agreed to take care of Honey while I was away.

After booking my Delta flight to Pittsburgh, I buried my face in my pillow. The tears I was expecting never arrived, which made me feel even worse than I was already feeling.

COURAGE OR LACK THEREOF

I woke up at 4 AM after sleeping only a few hours. After I quickly packed my suitcase, then suited up for a run on the cold damp Thanksgiving Atlanta morning. The rest of the city seemed to be sleeping as I ran down the empty streets with the aid of the streetlights. There was a cold drizzle combined with a slight breeze that kept sweeping across my face.

With each passing stride, I kept thinking that I was a coward. I left Pittsburgh for Georgia in the fall of 1996 to attend UGA. It was easy enough to justify my reasoning for leaving the city where I was born and raised. UGA offered me a full scholarship to run on their cross-country team, and shortly after the coach made the offer, I readily accepted. This was a great opportunity and one that I took full advantage of.

The truth of the matter though was that I had several other scholarships that would have kept me in Pennsylvania at reputable universities. Upon receiving my acceptance letter and offer, I phoned my grandfather and drove directly to his house to share the news.

After shaking my hand and congratulating me with a hug, he extended his hand to read the letter. He removed his eyeglasses and held the letter close to his wrinkled face. He squinted, studying each line of the letter and after he pulled the letter down, his eyes exploded with excitement followed by tears. He removed a handkerchief from his pants, or trousers as he would call them, to wipe the tears from his eyes.

"Matty, I'm so proud of you. You made this old man's day," he said.

Poppy was always my biggest fan as he shared each disappointment and each victory with me. There was even an occasion where he caused controversy at a race. He could care less about the official time because he kept the race times himself and always prided himself on being as accurate if not more so than the timekeeper.

In one state qualifying race, I finished second; however, the timekeeper's recorded time did not coincide with my grandfather's. According to Poppy's watch, I had run my best time of the year. My grandfather recorded all my race times and knew my race results better than I did. The course time that was recorded for me was different than Poppy's, which did not sit well with him. He waited until all the runners had finished until he decided to challenge the official results. There was a heated exchange between the two men after my grandfather questioned the man's ability and integrity. Some people might have been embarrassed by this type of exchange, but I came to recognize that this was who Poppy was and I admired him for his principles.

UGA was the first school to offer me a scholarship and as other offers came in, I shared those with Poppy. He reviewed the offers with me along with the journalism school rankings. He convinced me to accept the UGA offer because of the journalism school and the opportunity to move away from home and "become a man."

It was around this time that my grandfather had been diagnosed with cancer. I felt like I was running away from him because I could not bear watching him suffer. As one year transitioned into the next, I continually reassured myself that it was his idea for me to leave Pittsburgh. I think another reason that he suggested I leave was to protect my memories of him. He aimed to be remembered during his best years and not at the lowest point near the end of his life.

I arrived at the relatively empty airport shortly after seven. I use the term relatively because for Atlanta, the airport is typically a madhouse, but on this Thanksgiving morning, there were as few people there as I ever remember seeing. Granted, most of my travel occurs during peak times where I'm flying to the city where the Braves are playing away from home.

A Navy sailor stood behind me in line at Starbucks. The sailor reminded me of my grandfather, who enlisted in the

Army Air Force shortly after the Pearl Harbor attack. I insisted that I purchase whatever the serviceman wanted, knowing that not only was this the right thing to do, as this man was sacrificing his life for my freedom, but also because I knew that my grandfather would do the same.

My thoughts returned to the question of whether I was a coward, only this time it wasn't for leaving Pittsburgh. Poppy always encouraged me to attend one of the service academies. His preference of course was that I would enroll at the Air Force Academy. Did I let him down by not pursuing an academy, and was I a coward for not serving my country in such a capacity? These were questions that I never asked him, because I knew how he would have answered. The answer to the question was rooted in my own insecurity and had nothing to do with my grandfather.

I handed the Navy man his tall dark roast coffee and turkey bacon sandwich thanking him for his service. My thoughts returned to Poppy as I walked down the A terminal toward my gate. There was no one like him, and I knew there never would be anyone like him. Poppy had poor eyesight, and in order to get into the United States Army Air Force, there was a minimum requirement for the eye test. He knew that there was no way he could pass the eye exam so he convinced a friend to memorize the letters so that when it was his turn to take the test, he could merely recite the letters. This is exactly what he did, and as is often said, the rest is history. Poppy served as a bombardier in the United States Army Air Force in World War

II. Most of his time was spent in England, where his unit flew missions over Western Europe dropping bombs. Poppy flew thirty-five missions with the 8th Air Force and ultimately was awarded the nine-oak-leaf cluster air medal.

It felt like all I did was avoid the service and leave my ailing grandfather behind.

GOODBYE

My flight touched down at the Pittsburgh International Airport shortly after 9 AM. I loved this city. It was where I was born and grew up and there is always something special about returning to your roots. Your roots contain that special recipe which makes up your soul. It's a concoction of the land, culture, and family that make you who are, and that recipe cannot be replicated.

Still, I hated returning home under this circumstance.

I waited outside of baggage claim for about ten minutes before I noticed my brother Josh's hunter green Jeep Wrangler approaching.

"Welcome home big brother," said Josh as I opened the door to climb inside.

"Thank you for picking me up. I just wish the circumstances of my return were different."

"Poppy has been holding on just for you Matty," said Josh through tears.

I turned my face to stare outside the passenger window and bit down on my lip to hold back on the emotion that was building up inside of me.

"I'm not ready to say goodbye," I said.

"Once you see him you will be ready. He struggles with each breath and at this point, he basically exists now instead of actually living."

"How are Mom and Nanny doing?"

"About as well as they could be given the situation."

Normally, the drive from the airport to Monroeville flies by, but not on this day. As we drove east on I-376, I noticed details that I had never seen before, like the smooth white facade and the number floors of the Marriott in Findlay Township, or the number of buildings on the Covestro campus.

The sun was casting a brilliant glow off the PPG building and Monongahela River. We followed the river east toward the Squirrel Hill Tunnel when it suddenly dawned on me that this was Thanksgiving. I knew that today was Thanksgiving when I left Atlanta for Pittsburgh this morning, but I had long since forgotten. Thoughts of NFL games and turkey were the furthest thing from my mind right now.

Josh and I talked about our lives as he brought me up to speed on his family and I talked about Lana and her trial. I informed him about my desire to write a novel to which he said that it was about time, as he had heard me talk about the idea for years. We arrived at Forbes Regional hospital close to noon. Josh dropped me off on the front door after relaying Poppy's room number to me. He planned on returning home to have lunch and help his wife with the kids before coming back to the hospital later that afternoon.

I shook Josh's hand then climbed down out of the Jeep. I took a deep breath before walking toward the automatic sliding glass hospital doors. There was nothing more in the world that I hated than hospitals. The optimists of the world may take the glass-half-full approach when thinking about a hospital, considering that it is a place where many lives begin. Others could consider instances where their loved ones were cured of cancer and went on to live another twenty or thirty years.

I did not think in those terms though. For one, I had never been married nor had a child, so my perception of children entering the world was different than those that had. Any time I had been to a hospital, it was never for something positive. I lived through the death of multiple grandparents who developed cancer and, despite the best efforts of their doctors and nurses, never had the opportunity to live another twenty or thirty years. In each case, I lost both of my father's parents. My grandpap died when I was five and my grandma passed away nine years later when I was fifteen. Both contracted their cancers early in their fifties. They would never have the chance to see their grandchildren graduate from college and eventually get married.

God took them both early in life.

I stopped at the hospital gift shop to pick up a *Post-Gazette* for my grandfather, knowing how he loved reading the "papers." Poppy read several newspapers each day from front to back and completed the crossword puzzles in each paper. Occasionally, I would mail him copies of the articles I had written for the *New Atlanta Times* and the ones that I was most proud of. He attempted to read my paper online, but according to him reading news on a computer was not appealing. He was one of those people who liked the feel and texture of printed news. The sound of turning pages was part of the experience. I guess there is a part of me that understands his viewpoint.

Poppy gave me an appreciation for the papers, the way he had perfected the fold, never creasing the paper or making a mess of it. The way he had scolded me on several occasions when I was younger for folding the paper incorrectly. Despite working at the paper and reading print myself, I have yet to perfect the fold.

I took the elevator to the sixth floor and slowly walked down the cold lonely hallway towards his room. Never in my life have I encountered a hospital that was warm and welcoming. Even when I visited my brother and sister-in-law after their son was born, the hospital felt solemn. Perhaps the newborn wing has that type of feeling because the patrons or new fathers and mothers are running on fumes while they live in a state of sheer exhaustion not knowing what the future entails, which as I understand it, is many forthcoming sleepless nights.

I fought back tears when I stood at the entry door of Poppy's room. My mother and grandmother were sitting on opposite sides of the bed holding his hands. My mom and Nanny wept when I walked in. I will never forget the sight of all the tubes that were attached to my grandfather. He released his hands from my mother and grandmother's, lifting his arms toward his oldest grandson for one last embrace.

I leaned down and embraced him. He was a shell of his former self. I felt his ribs and spine. I remember never wanting to let go of him knowing that this could be the very last hug my grandfather and I would have. This was a big deal for me. I was never one for outward affection. Hugs were foreign to me. Weakness set in as Poppy dropped his arms and gasped for more oxygen than the breathing apparatus was currently delivering. He was attempting to speak to me.

"Matty, I'm so happy to see you. You made an old man's day today," he said.

"I'm sorry I didn't come sooner. More importantly, I'm sorry for leaving you and moving away."

"That's nonsense. I encouraged you to pursue your dreams, and you would have been foolish to pass up the opportunity to move to Georgia. No Matty, I have zero regrets, and you should not have any either. As I told you many times before, as the oldest grandson, you were always my favorite."

We talked for another twenty minutes about everything and anything. He reassured me that Lana would prevail and advised me to support her through every step of the trial. Poppy had the ability to view the world not only through his lens but also the lenses of those around him. From the time I discovered the charges against Lana until today, I never put myself in her place. Poppy was starting to fall asleep and asked me to come back later after he had rested.

My thoughts returned to Lana and for once, I attempted to look at her legal predicament from her point of view. Regardless of one's career or occupation, it takes years to establish credibility in an industry and within the company that employs you. Credibility and reputation can be destroyed within seconds despite the length of time it takes to establish oneself. Lana endured years of law school followed by countless hours in meetings, traveling, writing briefs, and executing mergers and acquisitions. She worked her way up in seniority to the point where becoming a partner was well within her grasp. Now she must have felt like all her efforts were for nothing. A single charge could erase almost two decades of effort.

I compared her situation to my own. What would it be like for me if I were to be charged with plagiarism? People would discount every single article I had written or questioned each story that I broke. My career would be ruined, and the chances were that I would never get another shot at chasing my dreams.

I found a nice quiet place in the hospital to phone Lana. I updated her on Poppy's condition but not before apologizing for not being more sympathetic for what she was going through. She graciously accepted my apology but quickly turned the focus back to me. Lana always invested more in everyone else than she did herself. Aside from my father, she was the most selfless person I knew.

Poppy was sound asleep when I returned to his room. My mom and Nanny were sitting next to each other when I walked in. They asked me if I wanted to join them for lunch in the cafeteria. I declined their offer because I had no appetite whatsoever. I pulled up a chair alongside Poppy's bed and started to think about all the great times I had with Poppy. Suddenly, he looked twenty years younger.

I hoped to remember the sixty-year-old version of him that I knew as a boy growing up, rather than the shell of his former self dying on a hospital bed. What always surprised me about Poppy was his strength. Physically, he and my father were the exact opposites—other than the fact they both stood at about the same height. Poppy was thin boned with narrow legs and arms. His build made him look much taller than he was. My dad, who spent forty-plus years in the construction industry, had a thicker bone structure with bulging forearms and biceps.

Poppy was fair skinned and always very well groomed. He looked and dressed the way I would imagine his English ancestors dressed. His thin balding gray hair was always neatly combed and unless the holidays were upon us, he was always clean shaven. I loved when he would grow his beard during Christmas time. He reminded me of a thin version of Santa Claus with his gray whiskers. Whiskers is how he referred to his scruffy gray holiday beard.

His daily attire was always selected by Nanny. I never thought to ask him why he had her select his clothes. I assumed because it was something she liked to do, and it made her feel good about herself. He always wore pants, or trousers as both Nanny and Poppy called them. Every pair of trousers looked the same. The only difference was the color of pants. On only the rarest occasions would he wear blue jeans, and when he did, he just seemed to look out of place. His typical attire consisted of long colored polyester pants, a white t-shirt, a short-sleeved collared shirt, and in most seasons, a sweater that he wore over the collared shirt. All his collared shirts had a breast pocket. That was an absolute must. Where else would he carry his pack of smokes? To complete his outfit, Nanny would always have a pair of colored socks which matched his pants and seasonal shoes.

I must have dozed off for an hour. Poppy had placed his cold wrinkled hand on my arm, which woke me up.

"Damn it. I'm sorry Matty, I didn't want to wake you."

"That's ok. I'm glad you did."

"Tell me Matty, what were you dreaming about?"

Unfortunately, I had no dream to share with him. Rarely do I ever have dreams, and when I do the memory of the dream is so vague that I can never really repeat what I had seen.

"I didn't have a dream."

"Can I tell you about mine?"

"Yes, please do."

"Have you seen my nurses?"

"The only one I have seen is the kind lady with the dark gray hair."

"Well, she's a genuinely nice woman, but that's not the one I'm referring to. The one I am talking about is much younger. She's probably in her late twenties with long blond hair and legs up to her shoulders."

"Poppy, I definitely have not seen that one then."

"Ok then. Let me tell you about my dream. I was flying my old plane, the Piper Cub, that I told you about."

"Yes, I remember. The plane you once had to land on the country road because you were running low on fuel and noticed the open road and a gas station."

"Good, you remember then. I will never forget the look on the people's faces when I pulled that plane into the gas station for a re-fuel, but anyhow. She was in the cockpit with me, and she had been drinking a bit. Well, she started to get a little frisky, but I am piloting a plane so there's no time for that, you know. At the same time, I looked over at her and my God, it was like looking at Helen of Troy."

Poppy always had a knack for storytelling. I preferred to hear stories about World War II over tales about his past girlfriends. Even as I grew older, I did not want to imagine my grandfather with anyone else other than Nanny. His stories were unforgettable though, and would have made for quite an interesting book. That was a story that only Poppy could have penned though.

"Poppy, where were you flying with this lady?"

"That's the thing, Matty. We were headed to the Cayman Islands when all of sudden, I heard gunfire."

"Do you think it had to do with flying B-52s in the war?"

"No. What was happening was that we were being mistaken for drug runners. You see, these type planes were known for running drugs in the Caribbean."

"So, what happened?"

"Well, we took some fire and I realized that my options were limited. I was either going to put her down or get shot down. I opted for setting the plane down and there was this wide open flat white sandy beach. I made sure my buxom passenger was tightly strapped in and then I glided the plane onto the beach. I'll leave the rest of the story to your imagination."

There was a knock at the door. Much to my surprise, Lana walked into the room with a bouquet of flowers. I do not know whose eyes lit up more, mine or Poppy's, as we both looked up at Lana. This was the second time in my life when Lana surprised me out of the blue by showing up without any indication.

The first time occurred when I was in New York City for a weekend series covering an interleague game between the Braves and the Yankees. I was sound asleep in my hotel room when the phone rang, and it was Lana. I tend to be grouchy when I am woken up, so I wasn't exactly friendly during our brief conversation. A little while later, I heard a knock at the door which for the second time that evening pulled me out of my REM cycle. I went to the door to discover that Lana had flown in to spend the weekend with me, and for the second time that night, I was less than friendly. This is one of the many moments where I wish I would have expressed my gratitude to her for making the effort and sacrifice to see me. Unfortunately, I acted more like Oscar the Grouch, or a cranky little five-year-old.

Lana entered the dimly lit hospital room and proceeded to hand the colorful flowers to my grandfather. She then crouched down to give him a hug. Poppy took a hold of her hand and motioned for me to come over as well. He then took my hand and placed it on hers and put both of our hands on his heart.

"Promise me this. I want you to promise me that you two will take care of each other no matter what. I am not going to make it to your wedding, but I will be there in spirit. If you keep me in your heart, I'll always be with you wherever you go."

Tears started to trickle down Poppy's cheeks and when I turned to Lana, I saw that all three of us were crying. I knew in my heart that he would not live long enough to attend the wedding and even if he had, there was no way for him to travel to Atlanta for the ceremony.

Poppy passed away on the Saturday right after Thanksgiving. With my mom, uncle, and my grandmother in the room, he died peacefully surrounded by the people who loved him the most. I knew the minute my mom's name appeared on my cell phone caller ID that Poppy was no longer with us.

An immediate peace came over me as I knew he would no longer suffer. There would be no more long nights where he painfully searched for oxygen to fill his lungs. There would no longer be the need for him to receive forceful pats on the back to loosen up the fluid in his lungs. All his pain and suffering had ended, but the mourning of his friends and family was just beginning.

Lana was nurturing and supportive, knowing the relationship that my grandfather and I shared. I was numb and in no state to communicate or even understand how I was feeling. Several years would pass before I felt the true impact of Poppy's death.

I was blessed to spend most of my formative years with both Nanny and Poppy. Some people never know their grandparents. God gave me the better part of a quarter century with them. There is no arguing the influence they had in shaping me. Without Poppy, I would have not heard a first-hand account of what it was like to fight for the United States in World War II. Even more so than all the generational history lessons he taught me, the most cherished thing I will take away from him is the way he loved me. Poppy loved his grandchildren without bounds, and for that I will be forever grateful.

Lana and I proceeded to the airport the day after the funeral. Days prior, I purchased a copy of the *Pittsburgh Post-Gazette*. I stuffed the paper in my backpack and waited for the opportunity to open to the obituary section. Lana had stepped away to buy coffee for the two of us and to make a few phone calls. My hands trembled as I turned to the section where I would find his name, Robert G. Welivar. There I was reading the obituary of a man who read this very newspaper daily for fifty plus years. Tears ran down my cheeks with each passing line starting with *Janice's beloved husband of 55 years*. Then came my uncle and mother's names followed by his long list of grandchildren. Next came his profession, Conrail railroad supervisor, followed by a few highlights of his military service in World War II.

I instantly began to hate the concept of an obituary. How could a paragraph of text tell the true story of an eighty-year-old man? A man who lost his father at the age of five in a tragic drowning accident. That detail was omitted. The reasons he elected to enlist in the US Army Air Force in the middle of collegiate studies at Colgate was also skipped over. I ached for pages of information describing the man who I looked up to and who along with my father shaped my life in many ways. I removed my yellow notepad from my pack and started penning a draft of what I would have liked to see in his obituary.

Robert George Welivar

Surrounded by family who loved him, Robert G. Welivar, more affectionately known as "Bob" to his wife and friends, "Dad" to his son and daughter, and "Poppy" to his grandchildren, has passed away. Born and raised in Williamsport, Pennsylvania, to Ralph and Helen Welivar, Bob outlived many of his friends, including those who served with him in World War II. Tragedy struck Robert at the age of five when his father passed away. Ralph Welivar drowned on a company boat outing in Louisiana. Robert's father did not know how to swim and ended up sacrificing his own life in order that women and children who were on the boat were saved first. He never mentioned to anyone that he could not swim and took it upon himself to ensure that women and children were the first to receive life preservers. Robert's fondest memories of his father were created at their home in Long Island, New York. Ralph was a serious man who graduated from Columbia University. He was working his way up the ladder in the gas company he worked for, and prior to his death he was the company Controller. Robert fondly recalled how their home had a wooden ledge that he would grab onto while his father walked underneath it. Ralph would leave his son hanging there until he could no longer hold and then he would catch him after his little boy let go. He was a strict and firm man who expected his son to behave. Ralph often disciplined Robert at the dinner table when he was not acting respectfully. Placing elbows on the table or not sitting up received a stern look from his mother and father alike. One can only imagine how different Robert's life would have been had his father lived. Chances are he would have stayed in the New York area attending school and university there. Fate eliminated that possibility.

Shortly after his father's death, Robert and his mother Helen moved to Williamsport where she had extended family. Robert would spend his childhood and young adulthood in the Lycoming County area. And Williamsport would be the town in which he would meet his future wife of fifty-five years, Janice Parr. Robert was a free spirit. Perhaps the freest of spirits. He looked up to an older boy who gave him the nickname Shadow. To his mother's chagrin, he would climb out of his bedroom window and sit on the roof. He loved to watch the people walking by on the street. This hobby provided a sense of freedom.

After graduating from Williamsport High School, he enrolled at Colgate University. Robert Welivar was a brilliant man, but he lacked structure and discipline. He recognized this and surmised that he would have possessed those qualities had his father lived. He was particularly gifted in mathematics. Computing complex addition, subtraction, multiplication, and division in his head came easy. Give him any set up of numbers and he could compute them. Despite his prowess for mathematics, he elected to study literature in college. His mother loved English literature. She was an avid reader and speaking and writing properly were paramount *to her. After completing his undergraduate degree in English Literature, Robert planned on eventually pursuing a law degree.*

His grades were inconsistent. He moved from the Dean's list one semester to probation during the next. Still, Robert enjoyed his early college years. He was a proud member of the Phi Kappa Tau. Years later he would point to his paddle which sat in the corner of his den. He liked to walk over and pick up the paddle and look over the names of boys inscribed on the four-foot-long piece of wood. His initiation always stuck with him. He painted a detailed picture of living in the fraternity house and how cold it was during the winter. He loved the feeling of the biting cold and the look of a foot of fresh fallen snow as he stared out his bedroom window overlooking the campus.

Robert loved going on adventures. One of the stories he loved to share was leaving Colgate to visit his girlfriend in Manhattan. He knew he was completely out of her league. Her parents neither approved nor disapproved of their relationship, but he knew they hoped she would end up marrying a family friend who attended an Ivy League School. Robert stood out like a sore thumb on his Manhattan trips. He was a typical college student with minimal finances and getting enough train fare to get to New York was a stretch. He laughed describing his "fashionably stylish" attire. On a particular trip he had forgotten to pack a belt, so he improvised by using a necktie in its place. This was not such a wise move for the boy who was trying to impress a well-to-do New York family as he pursued their daughter. The distance challenged their relationship and so did the war.

A patriot through and through with ancestors that served in both the Revolutionary and Civil War, like many in his generation, he quickly enlisted following the bombing of Pearl Harbor. The United States Army Air Force was the branch of the military he sought because he had a passion for becoming a pilot. With two years of college under his belt, he left Colgate. Truth be told, Robert G. Welivar had to find a creative path to be accepted into the USAF. Though his eyesight did not meet the minimum threshold, Robert did not let it stop him. He convinced a friend to memorize the eye chart and provide him with the letters used in the eye exam, which he passed. After training and flight school, Robert arrived in London, England, with a flight team of eight others. Their assignment was to fly their B-24 from England to bomb Germany. Robert's squad completed 35 separate missions. Although he aspired to be the pilot or co-pilot, Robert wound up being the bombardier for his squadron. He did get the opportunity to fly on practice runs when the flight crew would be practicing in England.

On a regular basis, Robert and his flight crew would return from their mission and learn that other crews had died that day. In World War II, bombers had a 20% chance of returning safely to the base from where they departed. Robert was eventually awarded the nine-oak-leaf cluster medal, which effectively represented receiving the medal nine times. He never spoke about the award to his children or grandchildren. Rarely would he describe the horrors of war, but when he did, his eyes conveyed the pain of losing friends. On one occasion, he described in detail the shell of a B-24 that had returned to England with only a few of the crew alive.

Bob left the military with the rank of first lieutenant. Like many of his generation, he always stayed in close contact and maintained a lifelong friendship with his crew. Shortly after returning to the United States after military R&R, Robert went back to Williamsport. He met Janice Parr and within two weeks they were married. A short time later, Janice became pregnant with their first child. Carl was born, and Robert returned to Colgate to complete his degree.

The young father with his newly minted degree started a photography business with a partner. The business was a big success and things were going so well that, in time, Robert had enough money to buy a Piper Cub Plane. Finally, he could live out his dream of being a pilot. He loved flying his Piper. One of his favorite stories is the time he noticed the fuel gauge was nearing empty. He was flying over a rural area in north central Pennsylvania. Robert spotted a gas station and a long straight road with no cars in insight. He gently guided his plane onto the two-lane road and pulled into the nearby gas station. After filling up, he waited long enough to make sure there were no cars around so we would have enough runway to get off the ground. His eyes conveyed a sense of pleasure telling that story and he recited it in such a way it felt as though you could see the movie version in your mind as he spoke the words.

Tragedy would strike again, unfortunately, when Robert's business partner took all the photography equipment and disappeared. The young husband and father was left with nothing and he needed to find a way to support his family. He found employment with Pennsylvania Railroad, which later became Conrail. He spent his entire career with Conrail, retiring after thirty-two years. He was a loyal and proud employee, but one could sense that he had regrets. He was extremely intelligent and never really lived up to his potential. He reflected on this fact often, noting that his father would have given him the guidance and discipline where he would have better utilized his gifts.

Six years after the birth of their son, Carl, Robert and Janice welcomed their daughter, Alice, into the world. The young family moved often during the early years. Conrail took them from Williamsport to Buffalo and then ultimately to Pittsburgh, where Carl and Alice would spend most of their formative years. Robert was proud of his children, often speaking about Carl's great athletic ability and Alice's kind heart. Losing his father at such a young age, Robert did not have much experience in knowing how to raise and mentor children. Again, something his generation rarely discussed were the challenges they had to overcome, like growing up without a father, or working through the post-traumatic stresses of war.

Robert and Janice fell in love with Ocean City, Maryland, or "the shore" as they referred to it. Every year they spent several weeks vacationing at the Ocean Mecca, which is a small motel located on the wooden boardwalk sandwiched between 22nd and 23rd Street. The two of them enjoyed their annual routine, spending time with old shore friends and eating breakfast at the Satellite Coffee Shop. They returned in late September with gifts for the kids, including Shriver's Saltwater Taffy.

A grandson or granddaughter could not have asked for a better grandfather than Poppy. He loved his grandchildren unconditionally and they had 100% of his attention when he was with them. He would spend most of his retirement years attending soccer and baseball games, wrestling matches, and dance recitals. His passion for both professional sports, as well as the sports activities of his grandchildren, was unmatched. He would curse out professional athletes as he simultaneously watched one game on television and listened to another on the AM/FM radio. Barry Bonds and Bobby Bonilla probably received the same amount of profanity from Jim Leyland as Bob threw at them while listening to the ball game on KDKA.

An eight-ounce bottle of Budweiser could also be found on the wire-table that sat next to his chair on the outdoor brick patio. The bricks were barely visible, because Janice and Bob covered the patio with a large outdoor rug that looked like AstroTurf.

Poppy did not reserve his sports commentary for only professional athletes. A missed penalty in a soccer game or a poorly called strike drew criticism of the referee or umpire officiating his grandchildren's games. On an occasion or two, he was kindly asked by the officiator to leave the field. He did so with grace, knowing that he crossed the line but also with the understanding that his point was delivered.

The hardest part of losing someone is watching them in their final years. There was nothing worse as Bob's wife, children, and grandchildren watched his condition deteriorate. By the end, he was a skeleton of himself, weighing less than ninety pounds. He required an oxygen tank to breathe. Aside from him, his grandchildren observed the hurt and pain on their mother's face as she cared for her dying father. They looked on while their mother helped her father to the bathroom and pounded on his back to loosen the fluid that was embedded in his lungs.

Alas, the day has arrived where we had to say goodbye to Robert Welivar. In some ways, we were grateful because we would no longer watch him suffer. He will always be our family's charming man with a great sense of humor. A man who loved his family and prioritized them. He will be remembered as an exceptional grandfather, father, husband, and friend. What this world has lost on this day, Heaven has gained.

As I finished writing the last sentence, I wiped the tears that ran down my cheeks before Lana had returned with two large cups of coffee. Suddenly, a peace overcame me as I felt that I was able to write what I could never verbally convey to him or anyone. Lana sat down and offered me a cup.

"Thank you, Lana."

"You're very welcome. How are you feeling?"

"Much better now."

I unzipped my backpack and handed her my notepad to read the letter. It was quite a while as she read—a kind of unbreakable silence that was refreshing, in a way. When she finished, and we started talking again, it was about something totally different.

THANKSGIVING IN DECEMBER

Lana and I returned to Atlanta shortly after the funeral. Her court case continued to progress with the first formal hearings scheduled after the New Year. Eddie's parents had gone back to the Philippines for Thanksgiving, so his family decided to celebrate once they returned home. This would be two firsts for me; Thanksgiving in December; and spending the day with the Romeros.

Eddie decided it would be a good idea to invite Daisy to his family's belated Thanksgiving dinner. When I suggested that it may be better if the two of them went out a few more times before coming home to mom and dad, he said, "Maybe, but I want to have home field advantage. Plus, with you and Lana there, it would be even better. The two of you can distract my dad."

"I see. So basically, this is all about you trying to get your mom's approval to date this girl."

He shrugged. "I can't date anyone that my mom doesn't approve of." On a warm Friday December evening—yes, Friday—the four of us piled into Eddie's four-door silver BMW X5. I guess all convention goes out the window when you make your own holiday schedule. It was obvious that Eddie and Daisy were only just starting to get to know one another.

"Eddie is this a hybrid?" she asked.

"No, they didn't have any hybrids available when I bought this."

I looked over at Lana who was seated next to me in the back and smiled. She raised her eyebrows, which was a signal for me to be quiet and not get involved in their conversation. We had just merged onto GA 400 North when Daisy asked, "Eddie, you told your parents that I'm a vegetarian right?"

"Yes, I called my parents the other day and told them."

Lana and Daisy chatted about growing up in Cobb County and playing soccer against one another. Their conversation helped pass the time and provided Eddie with some time to compose himself. I could sense his anxiety the way he tightly gripped the steering wheel.

I asked Eddie to exit at Old Milton so that we could stop at Whole Foods to pick up some wine. What a terrible decision that was. Avalon was beyond packed, and it took twenty minutes to find a parking space. The combination of the weekend, great weather, and Christmas season always drew people to Avalon.

We arrived at the Romero's suburban Alpharetta home a little late, but without issue. We were greeted by the Romero clan including mother, father, daughter, and grandparents. I felt overwhelmed standing there in the two-story foyer. I cannot imagine how Daisy must have felt being the featured guest of the evening. The nine of us moved from the foyer to the kitchen where we were offered drinks and appetizers.

Eddie's tiny grandfather was hilarious as he followed Daisy around and kept raising his eyebrows up and down. He reminded me of a Filipino version of Groucho Marx, minus the cigar. His wife, Eddie's grandmother, was even smaller than he was but extremely sweet. She watched her husband like a hawk as he playfully flirted with the girl his grandson was courting.

After all the proper introductions were made, we sat down at the dinner table. Grandfather Romero said grace as one would expect from a devout Catholic family. The nine-person dinner party was sizable, but the amount of food on the table could have easily served twenty. The patriarch and matriarch of the family sat opposite one another at the heads of the long wooden table. Lana and I were seated closest to Eddie's grandmother. Eddie and Daisy also sat on the same side of the table as us and Eddie's parents and sister sat across.

One serving dish after another was passed around the table. There were the traditional Thanksgiving staples, like turkey, stuffing, and mashed potatoes, as well as some Filipino foods like longganisa. I had always been a fast eater which quickly became a challenge because every time there was empty real estate on my plate, Eddie's grandmother quickly moved to fill it. I drastically slowed down my pace because there was no way I could continue to eat so much.

The conversation shifted to Daisy who cautiously worked to navigate around the dishes containing meat. Eddie's grandfather, who everyone referred to as Lolo, took notice of the stuffing on Daisy's plate.

"Daisy, I see you like the stuffing very much?"

Daisy answered, "Yes, it's delicious. Luckily, I do eat eggs, even though I am a vegetarian. I have never had stuffing that tastes so good. Is there a secret to your recipe?

"No dear, I just followed the Martha Stewart recipe," said Eddie's grandmother, Lola.

A wide grin appeared across Lolo's face. "I added the secret ingredient. When I tested the stuffing, it was too bland, so I added some small bacon pieces and grease from breakfast."

I looked at Lana who was already looking at me. It seemed like hours but within seconds the tension reached a boiling point.

"I told you that Daisy was vegetarian. She does not eat meat," scolded Eddie.

"Yes, that is why we made dishes for her without meat," said Lolo.

"Lolo, bacon is meat."

"No, bacon is from pig. Meat is from a cow."

"No, Lolo. Any food coming from an animal is meat. You're wrong," said Lola excitedly as she struck him with her white linen napkin.

"That's okay, Lolo," chimed in Daisy. "It's an honest mistake."

A look of relief came across Eddie's face as the intensity in the room transitioned away from code-red status. Lana elegantly shifted the conversation to the place in the Philippines where the Romeros came from. She always succeeded at steering things in a positive direction.

After Lana and I returned home, we concluded that this was one of our most fascinating Thanksgivings. We both decided that we would be eating lightly for the next several days. I cannot recall a time where my food intake was ever so great. Lola must have served me three pounds of food. The food was beyond delicious, save for the outrageous portions.

Wow.

Lana and I arrived back at her condo in the Eclipse around 10. Honey was dying for a walk after being home alone for so long, but I just didn't have the energy. I conceded for her benefit as well as my own. I traded my jeans for a soft gray pair of UGA sweatpants that I had since college. Lana joined Honey and me for a long peaceful December post-Thanksgiving walk.

It looked like Eddie and Daisy were off on the right foot after all.

JUST A KISS

A few weeks passed and Christmas 2019 was quickly approaching. I looked forward to spending the holidays and my week off with Lana. We planned a weeklong trip to the Cayman Islands a few days after Christmas. Lana had been preoccupied with her legal team with the looming February court date. She did well to compartmentalize all the stress and situation to the point where I had almost forgotten about the pending insider charges against her. My thoughts and feelings were starting to normalize as the weeks passed since my grandfather had died.

Then everything changed on a dime.

One evening, Lana and I were having dinner in her condo and the subject of her trial came up. I sensed something was weighing on her heart, so I pressed her to share what was bothering her. Tears started running down the sides of her cheeks as she gently placed her hand on top of mine. Instantly,

I knew something was wrong because Lana is not outwardly emotional. Only on the rarest of occasions have I seen her cry.

"Lana, what is bothering you. Please tell me."

She sniffled and collected herself before answering, "Matty, there is something I have to tell you. It's something that you are not going to like and it's going to hurt you."

"What is it, Lana?"

My heart started pounding through my chest as I nervously awaited her response. More tears came. I took my thumb and wiped the tears away from her cheeks.

"It's okay, Lana."

"Matty, what I am going to tell you is only part of the story. I cannot share everything because it is part of the case. Please trust me when I tell you that there is more to the story than what I am about to tell you."

"Lana, whatever it is, please tell me."

"Matty, I'm so sorry. Words cannot describe how sorry I am to tell you this."

"What Lana? What is it?"

I could feel my pounding heart in my ears.

"Matty, I'm sorry. I kissed Jack."

"What?"

"Yes, Matty, we kissed, but only once."

"When? Why? How could you?"

"It was in the summer after lunch one day. It meant nothing, and there's more to the story, but I cannot get into those details now, but I promise I will share everything with you when I can."

"Lana, I don't understand. First why you did this and second, why everything is so top secret. We are engaged to be married. Do you understand how much you just hurt me?" I stood up from my chair and began to excuse myself.

"Matty, wait, I want to talk about this. Most importantly, I love you."

I pushed in the chair. "I have to go. I need to be alone right now. I cannot. I just can't."

With that, I walked to the door and left. My legs were numb. I sat down in the stairwell, broken-hearted, unable to move or think.

Like many people, I had been cheated on before, just never by my fiancée. The idea of Lana and Jack kissing wouldn't leave my mind. There is no such thing as just a kiss. There always seems to be another endeavor that goes beyond the locking of lips. A kiss is a gateway. A kiss is tied to something deeper.

How could I ever trust Lana again? Was there something more going on beyond a kiss? Should I terminate the engagement?

A scarred heart may heal, but the scar will always remain, providing a constant reminder of the source of the scar. This was certainly not my first heartbreak, and most likely it would not be my last. The question I wrestled with the most circled back to trust. Trust takes time to develop but only seconds to destroy. I contemplated calling Lana to end our engagement, but something stopped me. I cannot describe what prevented me from calling her number or returning to her condo, but my conscience urged me to pause.

I needed to get away for a while, so I decided to take Honey out for a long run in the cold dark winter night. I looked down on her as she looked up at me with her long golden tail swinging swiftly. Honey was the most loyal friend I had. I took a knee and looked into her eyes. I wrapped my arms around her. That golden retriever will never know how much that hug meant to me. She walked over to the closet, retrieved her leash, and dropped it at my feet.

Did she know what I was feeling?

The run was consumed with me thinking about the justification for ending our relationship. Certainly, the combination of an insider trading criminal charge along with her kissing the other accused person would be more than enough for our parents and friends to understand. At the same time, what type of person leaves the person they are in love with at one of the lowest points of their life? I was in a no-win situation.

I returned to the conscience inside me that stopped me from taking any decisive actions. More than anything, I wished the night would end and I would wake up the next morning realizing this was all a bad dream. Unfortunately, I knew that my circumstances were more indeed my reality.

I anticipated a long sleepless night.

FORGOTTEN SHOEBOX

The next morning, I woke up craving a long run after such a heavy meal. Without a trim since October, I needed a hat to keep my hair out of my eyes when I ran.

When was the last time I wore a hat?

I had no recollection. College, maybe? That was twenty years ago. Right around the time my beloved Pirates began their decades-long fall from the top. It got so bad that I adopted the Boston Red Sox as my American League team. Naturally, I bought myself a trusty Red Sox cap.

In searching for it, I came across an old forgotten shoebox. The box was layered in dust, having been left untouched for years. Inside, I found a collection of old photos, stories, cards from family, poems, plus concert and movie ticket stubs.

The prospect of a morning run faded as, one by one, I removed memories from the box. I did not intend to spend the morning revisiting my past . . .

It was obvious from the dates of the tickets and those at the top right corner of handwritten poems that I had started filling the box shortly after arriving in Georgia for college. There were no high school photos or memorabilia. I could only guess that my pre-college shoebox must have still been at my parents' house in Pittsburgh or packed away somewhere in the back of my closet.

Better leave it there, I thought. Wherever it is.

I had my hands full with this forgotten shoebox, anyway. The first picture I came across was taken at Centennial Park, back when people still took film rolls to pharmacies to be developed. In the 2001 timestamped photograph, the sun was setting in the distance as my friends David, John, and I stood in front of the stage at a BTE show. Above the stage was the signage for the *On the Bricks* summer concert series. I recall that summer very well for several reasons. First, I was excited and terrified at the same time because I had just arrived in Atlanta. The cross-country team started training several months before the fall semester began. Like others on the team, I was hundreds of miles from home and unfamiliar with the South.

Luckily for me, I quickly became friends with John, a junior who hailed from the Constitution State (also the Nutmeg State, as he liked to remind us). We both stood out amongst our peers with our "thick" northern accents. John was the first one to warn me about the humidity, and he was not kidding. My August in Georgia was torturous.

John quickly developed into the older brother that I never had growing up. When we had free weekends, he would take me sailing on his 1984 Hobie Cat sailboat. I never sailed before but quickly fell in love with the feeling of the speed as the light blue sails filled up with the swift Lake Lanier winds. On the days where there was no wind, John shifted from sailing to water skiing. His girlfriend, Cindy, was always happy to take us out on her parents' red Mastercraft ski boat. John was equally as talented at water skiing as he was at sailing.

I sighed and smiled thinking back to those days as I moved on to other pictures. I missed John and Cindy, and knew I needed to work harder to stay in touch with them. After graduating from UGA, they married and moved to Ohio where John landed a job working in public relations for the Columbus Blue Jackets.

Those were fifteen-year-old memories.

I glanced back down at the photograph of David. Throughout our four years of college, David and I spent a great deal of time traveling all over the southeast to see our favorite bands. Four-hour drives across the Tennessee, South Carolina, and Alabama state lines were commonplace. On certain occasions, we would make the eight-hour drive to New Orleans during Mardi Gras. Many of our favorite bands played on or near college campuses, and we often joked that we spent more time on the campuses of other colleges than we did at Athens.

David and I saw Better than Ezra at Auburn, Matt Nathanson in Birmingham at the Workplay Theater in 2002, Roger Clyne and the Peacemakers at Smith's Olde Bar in Atlanta. No matter what campus we visited, or what the architecture looked like, we always seemed to hear the same soundtrack. It did not matter if you were at Vanderbilt, Georgia Tech, or Ole Miss. Jason Mraz's "The Remedy" and John Mayer's "Your Body is a Wonderland" were in constant rotation along with older songs like Barenaked Ladies' "Brian Wilson," Blink 182's "What's My Age Again," and Semisonic's "Closing Time."

In some ways I envied the people who spent all their time on their own college campuses, because they developed much deeper relationships and friendships than I did at the time. Still, I have always been too much of a restless spirit to go through the rinse, wash, repeat weekly cycle where a typical student goes to class Monday through Friday but starts their partying on Thursday and begins the weekend recovery on Sunday. On more than one occasion David and I found ourselves approaching the Welcome to Georgia sign at some odd hour, on some odd day, with Better than Ezra's "At the Stars" playing in the background. The stars always seemed to show us the way as we drove east on I-20 towards Atlanta.

For whatever reason, I craved the feeling of being right on the edge of experiencing something but not close enough to be attached to the experience. The deeply personal lyrics from Smashing Pumpkins' "Mayonaise" have always resonated with me.

From the shoebox I fished out the photos of my 2003 cross-country road trip. This was a trip I took alone, but not because I wanted to be alone. My friends and brothers were either working with their newly minted college degrees or they had other summer commitments. The girl who would have accompanied me on this journey across the United States was out of the picture. I knew that my job at the *New Atlanta Times* would not provide the opportunity to get away so easily.

So, I packed my black 1999 Chevy Cavalier (no air conditioner) with a backpack full of jeans, t-shirts, and shorts, along with two loaves of bread, peanut butter, and two cases of bottled water. The pictures, gas and hotel receipts, and national park passes tell the story of the trip much better than I could ever articulate. The ten-day journey commenced in late July on Tuesday, the 22nd day of the month. Two pages of loose-leaf handwritten with directions on both the front and back pages sat adjacent to me on the dark gray clothed passenger seat—the same two pages I was looking at now. The first destination, Sedona, Arizona, was 2,041 miles away.

I remember driving for about six hundred miles before pulling into a dimly lit truck stop off the highway to sleep. I spent the majority of the next day driving through pancake-flat Texas until I reached the point of exhaustion and checked into the Pony Soldier Motel in Tucumcari, New Mexico. A room was cheap enough for the $800 I'd budgeted for the entire trip (including hotels, gas, national park fees, and food).

That morning, I left The Pony Soldier Motel before dawn. I watched the sunrise from the driver's seat of my 1999 cavy. My first stop was the Petrified National Forest and the Agate Bridge. From there, Painted Desert stretching red and proud out to the edges of the horizon. Then Meteor Crater off Highway 40, the 50,000-year-old bowl that can't be captured in a single camera shot.

Finally, I reached Sedona.

Since that trip, many people have asked me if I was lonely as I traversed the country alone. Maybe when I was driving. But there's a presence and a power in each of the places I visited, something that remained with me until the next destination.

I continued thumbing through the pictures in the shoebox. The winding roads and red rocks of Sedona. The expansiveness of the Grand Canyon, which made the Colorado River look like a stream. I have vivid memories of this section of my journey. I spent countless hours circling back to the summer relationship I had a few years back with a girl named Lexie. Lexie and I met during the summer of 2003 in Destin, Florida. Through a family friend, I landed a bartending job at Pompano Joe's. I felt like I had won the lottery that summer. While most of my peers desired to work summer jobs at the beach, I actually had the fortune of working on the beach. Others my age landed jobs in the outlets at pizza shops or retailers.

It was love at first sight for me when my eyes first fell upon Lexie. I was assigned the outdoor bar and on my second day of employment, there she was, serving a family of four. The husband, wife, and two young boys were seated on the outside deck with a brilliant orange painted wooden exterior complete with yellow, pink, and green umbrellas. At one point a customer woke me from my trance because my eyes were glued to her. Lexie's long chestnut hair swirled around her cheeks as she moved from one table to the next. Our paths crossed later in the afternoon when she approached the bar. I felt like I was going to drown in her turquoise eyes. I casually filled her drink order, placing two pina coladas onto her serving tray.

For two days we went through this routine where she would provide an order and I would fill it. This went on until I finally mustered up the courage to introduce myself. That was the beginning of a two-month summer relationship. The two of us were inseparable, spending all our free time at the beach. Lexie and I must have covered hundreds of miles walking along the white powdery shores of the Gulf of Mexico. Rarely did we eat out at the classic Destin establishments like the Crab Trap or McGuire's. In order to save money, we lived on grilled cheese and peanuts. Our nightly treat was Cuban coffee. Lexie prided herself on using her maternal grandmother, Alexandra's recipe. Other than the twenty dollars she arrived with when she immigrated from Cuba to Florida in the 1950s, Lexie's *abuela* brought little beyond the clothes she was wearing and the memories of the traditions and recipes that were passed along to her from previous generations. Lexie's eyes lit up when she prepared the super-sweet coffee. All these years later I can still recall the sweetness of the sugar on my lips.

We worked to avoid the inevitable fact that the end of summer would result in my returning to Athens, Georgia, and her to Gainesville, Florida. Lexie was highly intelligent, and most of the time I was completely lost when she spoke. She was a Chemical Engineering major with plans to pursue a medical degree. What impressed me most about Lexie was what inspired her academic pursuits. Both of her grandparents died of cancer in their fifties. Lexie had an insatiable thirst for knowledge where she wanted to learn everything from how a drug was synthesized to how they were manufactured. That was the basis of her pursuit of the engineering degree. With a foundation in engineering and chemistry, her goal was to learn about the drugs or technology that interacted with the body, with the final goal of working to find a cure for cancer. Lexie was unlike anyone I had ever met or encountered.

And then the moments together that seemed like summer movie scenes faded. We parted and that was that.

I exhaled as I spent a few extra moments looking at a photograph of us seated in the lifeguard's chair together. I was seated with my back against the tall sundrenched white wooden chair while she sat in front of me. The sun was setting behind us while we looked at the emerald water. For a brief minute, my thoughts drifted back and forth comparing the relationship I had with Lexie to my relationship with Lana. Maybe the comparison was unfair. With Lana, I had discovered my soulmate. Lana understood me better than I understood myself. I also met Lana at a different stage of life. Still, there is something about those old summer loves.

I never really moved on until I reached the Grand Canyon that summer. Gazing out at the greatness and depth of the red rocks and cliffs, I let her go. It seemed so easy and simple. Had I known that the Grand Canyon would heal my broken heart, I would have made the trip much sooner.

To this day, every time I hear the song "Only You" by Yaz, the lyrics transport me back to that summer with Lexie. For the longest time until I fell into a new relationship a few years later, I hung on to those poetic lyrics.

With each flip from photo to photo, I missed the nostalgia of actual photographs. Digital images are fantastic and can be pulled up instantly with a Google search or in an iPhone's library, but they just are not quite as intimate as feeling the glass of a picture between your fingers.

From the Grand Canyon, my journey continued to Los Angeles—from the desert to a crowded city and the ocean. I experienced the coldness of the Pacific for the first time when I dipped my feet into the water at Santa Monica Beach. Touring

Los Angeles felt just like walking through the scenes of a Hollywood movie only on a smaller scale. Instantly, I knew I did not fit into the Beverly Hills scene with my old worn t-shirts and jeans. From Los Angeles, I headed north to Yosemite National Park. Arriving just before nightfall, I had no room or accommodations for the evening. For the second time on the trip, I spent the evening in the back seat of my car, which was parked in a lot near the Wawona Hotel. There was no way I could have stayed in the hotel. The next morning, I woke up well before sunrise and started driving to see the majesty of El Capitan and Half Dome. I stood amazed while I took in the six hundred-plus foot Bridalveil Fall. To this day, I have never experienced a beauty or purity like Yosemite.

The next day I went to San Francisco. Upon driving into the city, I found a parking spot near Fisherman's Wharf, ditched the car, and trekked up and down the hills all the way up to Coit Tower then back over to Lombard Street. I began to fall in love with the sounds of the trolley cars, the smell of the fresh air swirling off the bay, and the amazing architecture. By the time I crossed the Golden Gate Bridge, the city behind me had stolen a piece of my heart.

That imagery sustained me all the way to Ashland, Oregon, where I pulled off the road and checked into the Vista Motel, where I must have been feeling all those miles in the car, because the next pictures in the shoebox were a few scarce shots of Portland and Seattle.

From there, the trip becomes a whirlwind in my mind. Saltese, Montana, after ten hours of driving. The Highway 89 marker next to a wooden sign with the words, "Welcome to Gardiner, Montana: Original Entrance to Yellowstone Park." The Snake River and the lingering smell of sulfur spewing out from the steaming pools. In Greybull, Wyoming, I bought my first meal of the trip—a double cheeseburger and root beer at A&W. That was calories enough to make it to Mount Rushmore, then Sterling Motel in Austin, Minnesota—last stop before Pittsburgh. I can still picture that red and orange on the horizon behind me, with Tracy Chapman singing "Fast Car" on the radio as I neared my parents' home.

My journey of self-discovery had come to an end.

I glanced at my watch, discovering that I had spent the last three hours reminiscing about my past. I looked at one last picture.

It was a photograph of Skylar. I closed the shoebox and placed the picture of Skylar in my dresser drawer. I knew I had to revisit that relationship one day.

Just not now.

EGGSHELLS & COVID-19

Three days passed until I finally mustered up the energy to see Lana again. We both walked on eggshells with neither of us wanting to revisit the subject of her kissing Jack. The pain in my heart was numbing but it was too raw to deal with, and she could sense the way I was feeling. So, we tiptoed.

Over the next few weeks, we spent more time talking about baseball than we did during our entire three years of dating. But it was obvious to me that she had little interest in the 2020 Atlanta Braves. Soon, we ran out of "safe" topics and needed some time apart. Luckily, spring training provided us with that opportunity. In previous years, Lana would join me for at least a week in Florida. I would spend an entire month starting in mid-February through the final games in mid-March before returning to Atlanta for the regular season. This year would be different though. Lana could not get away because of the amount of time she was spending with the lawyers in preparing for her trial. Given what happened with Jack, I'm not sure I'd want her there if she could.

I arrived in North Port, Florida, under quite different circumstances than in previous years. Like most people, there were expectations that 2020 would be a roller coaster of a year with the presidential election in November; but combined with the news of a quickly spreading pandemic, there was an eerie feeling that surrounded us. No one knew or could comprehend what was going to happen next. It felt like we were all walking on eggshells in North Port, too. By March 12, Major League Baseball cancelled all the remaining Spring Training games and delayed Opening Day by two weeks. With the ending of spring training, I boarded the Delta flight back to Atlanta along with others in the press corps.

Sitting at the Ft. Meyers airport terminal, I got a premonition that life would soon change.

An entire new vocabulary was being introduced to people around the world. Suddenly, people began talking about COVID-19. What initially was being described as a version of the flu, COVID took on a much more dramatic meaning. New social norms were being deployed to protect the health and safety of the masses. Explicit instructions were given on how to wash one's hands, socially distance, and wear protective masks.

By mid-March, most nations around the world were in lockdown. For the most fortunate among us, lockdown translated into working from home while limiting any travel outside of the home except for a trip to the grocery store. Although COVID-19 had no dysentery symptoms, droves of Americans started hoarding toilet paper. The shelves of Publix, Kroger, Target, and Walmart were completely empty. For the first time in my life, the metallic shelves lining the aisles were mostly empty. Beyond toilet paper, tissues, paper towels, soap and any type of disinfectants, soup, pasta, and water were soon the rarest of commodities.

People were glued to their televisions and social media, watching the daily ticker of COVID-19 cases and deaths, all of it increasing without an end in sight. People became instant health professional experts studying the statistics and working together to "bend the curve." After some time spent wondering what to do, Lana proposed that I shelter in place with her family in Milton, Georgia. Daisy and Eddie had been together for a few months and now she planned to move in with him during the lockdown. The prospect of living in such a small place with Eddie, Daisy, and Honey seemed challenging, so I took Lana up on her offer. I packed my suitcase, a backpack, my laptop, and Honey's food and dog bowls. When I opened my dresser drawer to get my Timex running watch, I stumbled across the picture of Skylar. I took the photo and placed it inside my copy of *The Sun Also Rises*. Many years had passed since I had read a novel recreationally. I figured Hemingway was a good place to start.

Eddie and I bid farewell not knowing when we would see each other again. It felt like a forever goodbye. Neither one of us was emotional, but I could sense he felt the same way I did. After Eddie closed the door, I stood with Honey in the hallway, just taking a few minutes to reflect on what was transpiring.

Lana met Honey and me in the parking garage. I packed the Prius and followed behind her black Audi A6. We discussed taking one car, but neither one of us knew how long this would last or what the end game would be—not for the world, nor for us.

MILTON, GEORGIA

For the first time in a long time, I felt alone. Even though I was going to stay with Lana, my relationship with her was hanging on by a thread. Sitting alongside me in the passenger seat, Honey was excited about our northbound adventure. The traffic on Georgia 400 seemed typical, but I assumed this was the result of other migrants moving to their desired lockdown location. I noted the different license plates of my fellow travelers. There were several from Florida, a few from Tennessee, both Carolinas, New York, and even my native Pennsylvania.

I dreaded the thought of how awkward it would be around Lana and her parents given the circumstances of our relationship hurdles. I enjoyed spending time with Mr. and Mrs. Trangate, but I had never spent an extended period with them. Certainly not under such strained circumstances. Milton, Georgia, is situated at the northernmost part of Fulton County bordering Cherokee county and is one of the few places remaining in the northern suburbs of Atlanta that is fighting to remain "horse country." The drive from Buckhead to Milton reminded me of an old summer commercial of a kid riding their bike through rolling country fields with wildflowers. Within forty-five minutes, both city and suburb were behind me.

The Trangates lived on a large five-acre estate on Providence Road. I pulled into their long winding driveway, which was lined with cherry trees planted just opposite each other. The expansive gray painted brick home combined the look of a modern farmhouse with a touch of a European chateau. Standing atop a hill, the house was L-shaped, with the main home extending horizontally toward the garage, above which a large office and guest room were built. The garage portion of the house reminded me of the Seaver family home in *Growing Pains*.

Mr. Trangate stood at the top of the driveway where he pointed me towards the one open garage door of the four available bays. Honey squealed in delight. She loved Lana's parents' home because they had a large fenced-in backyard where she could run freely all day long. She knew exactly where we were and could not wait to get out of the car. Mr. Trangate followed me into the garage, taking Honey off my hands while welcoming me.

"Hello Matty, it's great to see you."

"Thanks Mr. Trangate. Likewise. Thank you so much for letting me ride out the lockdown at your home."

"You're very welcome, and please stay as long as you like. Matty, Mrs. Trangate has set up the basement for you so you will have your privacy down there. Please make yourself at home and use the kitchen as freely as you like. The bar, too, but if you decide to have a bourbon or scotch, please let me know so I can join you."

"Thank you, sir. Will do."

"Also, we moved Mrs. Trangate's office upstairs so you can use hers in the basement."

"Thank you again, but you didn't have to do that. I don't want to impose on you all."

"Of course not, it's our pleasure Matty. Say, after you drop off your bags and get washed up, how would you like to go for a walk with me?"

"Sure, that would be nice."

I proceeded inside while Mr. Trangate took Honey around back to the yard. No one else was inside, so I took my suitcase downstairs to the bedroom. I took a deep breath looking across the never-ending finished basement. The bottom level of their home was massive, probably four times the square footage of Eddie's condo. The light colors of the ash hardwoods created a beach-like feeling. Large sliding glass doors opened out to the inground heated saltwater pool. I slid open the doors, glancing out at the lush green rolling landscape which eventually dropped to a small lake at the back of the property. I shook my head just thinking about how I could never provide even a fraction of this lifestyle to Lana. The two of us never spent much time talking about our long-term plans. We agreed that after we were married, I would move into her Buckhead condo and the conversation never went any further. We planned on having kids, but not immediately, so there was no need to explore our future lives, I guess. And now it was all up in the air.

I spotted Mr. Trangate out in the yard throwing a tennis ball for Honey. Mr. Trangate could be cast as a J. Crew model, really. He had a tall, lean build and his charcoal gray hair was always neatly combed, his chiseled face cleanly shaven. Mr. Trangate wore Tom Ford glasses with black metal rims and clear lenses. In all the years I knew him, I never once saw him wear jeans. His casual attire consisted of four rotating colors of chinos, which he always wore with a button-up shirt. Come to think of it, I never saw him wear a t-shirt either. He was always well put together and fit, the latter a result of his love of cycling and swimming, I gathered. According to Lana, he could not stand running.

Both Mr. and Mrs. Trangate achieved great success in their careers. He was the director of sales for Oracle, and she was a partner at Bain and Company. Their four children, three boys and Lana, were also extraordinarily successful. Two of their sons practiced medicine, while both Lana and her youngest brother were rising lawyers in their respective firms. Mr. Trangate was a natural salesman. He approached me and placed his arm around my shoulder. I envied his gravitas. He had a voice and tone and balance to his speech that could have furnished him a career in radio or television. The two of us started down the long steep driveway.

"I hope you're not too busy today, Matty. If you do not have time now, we can take a walk later."

"No, I'm free. It's Saturday and the 2020 baseball season is on hold indefinitely, so I have time."

The bright spring sunshine was blinding and unlike Mr. Trangate, who was already wearing his aviator shades, I had none, so I squinted. There was awkward silence between us as we continued to descend the winding concrete driveway. I decided to break the silence. "Mr. Trangate, you have such a beautiful home. I cannot tell you how much I appreciate your hospitality."

As we continued to walk, he unbuttoned the cuffs on his shirt sleeves and rolled them up to his elbows. He removed his sunglasses and looked directly into my eyes. I cannot imagine that he could not sense my anxiety as I anticipated his next sentence.

"Matty, I'm going to share something personal with you. All right?"

"Yes sir," I replied.

"Appearances can be deceptive. You probably look at this house and are struck by how much money we have. That is not the case. We have a massive mortgage on this home and owe far more than the equity we have in it."

"I would never guess that."

Mr. Trangate continued. "This outward lifestyle of a large estate along with expensive cars are all part of a facade that Mrs. Trangate and I use to entertain our clients. When you are working on multi-million-dollar deals, you need to portray a certain persona. With that portrayal of success comes a lot of debt, because the forward-looking image requires a package of expensive furniture, home décor, the pool, and any other intricate item you can imagine in a Pottery Barn store. What I am saying is this is not who we are, and this outward lifestyle does not represent the two of us. Lena and I are playing a role like an actor or actress would."

We were silent awhile, which afforded my mind the chance to drift. I was reminded of the performance enhancing drugs era in baseball. The 1990s through early 2000s produced an abundance of home run hitters who were averaging more than forty home runs each year. Until the steroid news, or more specifically the PEDs story broke, people did not link the performance of the players to the drugs. It was all a big, entertaining, unprecedented show—all over-inflated because of the drugs. Once the scandal broke and regulations were put in place, the home run totals dipped. As a baseball purist, I hated this time period. Within a span of ten years, the records held by the likes of Hank Aaron and Roger Maris had fallen to . . . cheaters.

"Matty, I want you to know that Lana shared something personal with my wife and me. She told us about what's-his-name. She also told us it was not what it appeared to be, and that she'd tell you all about it once the timing was better.

"Matty, I believe my daughter. She is honest and she loves you. I trust her, and I hope you do too. I can understand how hurt you were when you learned about this, and rightfully so. I would feel the same way if I were in your position. At the same time, if you love Lana, then you need to trust her. I recognize that I have overstepped my bounds here. I fully get that. I just want you to give Lana the chance to share more and not risk everything the two of you have. At least not yet."

There I was utterly speechless. How could I possibly respond or say anything? My deepest hope was that he would change the subject and do so quickly. I could not bear any more. Here I was living out Ben Stiller's character in *Meet the Parents*. I had no desire to enter the "circle of trust," rather preferring to operate on a need-to-know basis. The wealth, or lack thereof, of my future in-laws was none of my business and I am rarely one to have deeply personal conversations with others. I needed to change the subject quickly.

"Mr. Trangate, do you have any plans or things you would like to do while we are all quarantined?"

"Funny you should ask, because Lena and I just had this discussion over breakfast this morning."

"Really, what did you decide on?"

"We actually wanted to start planning out our retirement. Ten years from now we both plan on exiting the rat race and would love to downsize and move to a small home in a sleepy Florida beach town."

"Something like Seaside or Alys Beach?"

"Maybe, you know we have never been anywhere on the gulf coast except Destin and Ft. Walton. We took the kids there ever since they could walk, and that became our annual vacation spot. Over the years, we developed such a routine, always renting the same house in Frangista Beach. With that we frequented our favorite restaurants and never deviated. I know it's not overly exciting to hear, but some of our best family memories originated on those powdery beaches."

"Retirement is so far for me that it's something I never think about," I replied.

"Well, Matty, the years will fly by, especially after you and Lana have children. The days and nights will be long, but the years will be short."

"Is there anything else you would like to accomplish when you are home during this period?"

"We plan on catching up on movies and even reading. I cannot tell you the last time I read a recreational book. Beyond that Matty, I don't yet."

The next hour or so as we walked, we covered a range of topics that are typical of small talk between a future son-in-law and their future in-law. We discussed sports and how different the 2020 seasons were going to be. We talked about the horse farms adjacent to their house, and old friends we both had not spoken to in years but hoped to catch up with.

Later in the evening I tasted Jefferson's Ocean Bourbon. Lana provided me with the origins of Mr. Trangate's Tuesday night bourbon tradition. Since its inaugural season of 2003, Mr. Trangate has watched every episode of *NCIS*. He fashions himself to be like one of the lead characters, Leroy Jethro Gibbs. Despite being told by wife and daughter alike that he lacks the hypermasculinity of the main character, Mr. Trangate always seems to find at least one parallel between himself and the main character. With no military background whatsoever, the only similarities I succeeded in identifying was their hair color, gray or silver, aging eyesight which requires eyeglasses, and a penchant for bourbon. Mrs. Trangate let me in on a little secret when Mr. Trangate took a bathroom break during a commercial.

He only started drinking bourbon after watching the show.

Suffice it to say that at the end of the show Gibbs removed an old dusty glass filled with bolts and screws from a wooden shelf in his basement. Then he took the bottle of bourbon sitting on top of his workbench and poured it into the dirty glass, took a sip, then set down his glass before beginning to sand the hull of a wooden boat there in his basement.

Mr. Trangate grinned as though he was working alongside Gibbs. Immediately I understood the appeal. Gibbs and his bourbon represented the old-school version of a man's man. A modern-day Clint Eastwood with a tough exterior and ruggedness. I never did quite acquire the taste for the aged ocean bourbon, but for the month or so I joined Mr. Trangate for the Tuesday night ritual.

Not quite man enough, I guess.

OLD SOULS

If I'm being honest with myself, my initial attraction to Lana was purely physical. Within a short period of time though, I discovered that beyond her physical beauty, Lana was not only brilliant, but kind and I loved the old soul in her. Lana possessed wisdom uncommon to someone in their thirties. She was grounded in her beliefs and world outlook. Lana never spoke an ill word or thought about anyone as long as I had known her, and she always found a way to see the best in people.

One of the last things I did before leaving the Buckhead condo was collect my mail from the kitchen countertop where Eddie developed a filing system which separated his mail from mine. I had officially taken up residence in Milton at least for the foreseeable next few months. Gradually, I began to return to more normalized routines like going through mail and paying bills.

In the process of sifting through my mail pile, I arrived at a handwritten letter from Lana. The two of us used to frequently write letters to each other in the early stage of our relationship. Lana enjoyed this type of old school formal communication. Many of our correspondences occurred in the summer months when I was on the road during baseball season. I too loved receiving Lana's letters which she penned in perfectly written cursive.

I carefully unsealed the light blue envelope. There were several pages neatly folded and packed inside. My heart began to race in anticipation.

Dear Matty,

It's been so long since I've written that I am ashamed of it. I apologize for not sharing my feelings with you more often. Too many times, I simply assume that you know exactly how and what my heart is feeling.

This is by far the most difficult letter that I have ever written to you. My heart trembles with each passing sentence because for the first time in our relationship, I feel like I have hurt you and let you down. Even if it's unintentional, I see the pain on your face when we are together.

I understand that I'm being unfair to you by asking you to trust and believe me concerning all the events involving Jack. And that is exactly what I am doing again. Please Matty, trust me when I say that you are the love of my life. I would never do anything to jeopardize that love.

I am obligated by law, confidentiality, and the ongoing legal proceedings not to disclose the details of the case. What I will share with you is that if you are willing to trust me and believe me, everything will become clear once the trial starts to unfold. There is nothing for you to worry or be concerned about. I promise you with all my heart that I have remained loyal to you and never had any physical relationship with Jack.

Matty, I also want to thank you. Thank you for respecting my wishes to wait until we are married. You have never pressured me and for this I am grateful.

I also want to express my gratitude for your patience. Thank you for accompanying me to company parties and non-profit events. You do this for me even though there are countless things you would prefer to do instead.

I appreciate how you supported me when I became a big sister in the Big Sisters of America Organization. Without hesitation, you attend my niece's dance recitals (although I'm convinced that you have discovered a way to sleep with your eyes open).

Lastly, thank you for agreeing to stay at my parents' home during the COVID lockdown and to work on repairing our strained relationship. This means more to me than you know.

I love you with all my heart and look forward to spending the rest of our lives together.

Love,

Lana

XOXOXO

CABLE NEWS & CHAIN SMOKING

Two weeks into the pandemic I soon realized that I could no longer bear watching cable news. With the endless rising death tolls and finger pointing, I had enough. Initially, I joined the Trangates in their great room every night, but the scrolling words and death counts reminded me of CNBC where they show the daily values of the Dow, S&P, and Nasdaq on the right side of the television screen and run the stock prices across the bottom. The nation had quickly transformed, now awash with so-called "health experts." I am a sportswriter and the boundaries of my expertise do not expand much beyond baseball and the metrics. I know batting average, slugging percentage, and earned run average. I know the ins and outs, the nuance, the historic norms. Suddenly, my peers in news broadcasting had become similarly well-versed in the inner workings of a pandemic.

And the meteorologists were analyzing football.

The sports anchors were sharing new recipes.

And the politicians? The president didn't sound like an expert, either. That 2020 was an election year only made it worse, especially given the choice between two senior citizens.

The perfect storm of chaos was playing out daily.

Even worse than hearing clueless politicians and journalists spout on about COVID was the families who were losing loved ones. Daily, the most vulnerable people around the world who contracted COVID were dying. Amid that tragedy, the typical means of mourning were not allowed. Then there were the folks losing their jobs. Terminology continued to be introduced with words like furlough. Furlough, a word that has been around well before the 21st century, started to become used regularly. Friends and family members in the service industries were being laid off. As the weeks wore on many restaurants and small business retailers were going out of business.

So, I decided to skip the news and pick up smoking again.

There was a short period of my life where I experimented with smoking cigarettes. It was during the summer when I met Lexie. Neither one of us had ever smoked a cigarette before, but for a period of two weeks we became chain smokers.

We were inspired for the silliest reason.

There was this older couple that sat on a blanket not far from the outdoor Pompano bar where I was working at the time. The gray-haired couple would listen to their old-fashioned handheld radio complete with dual cassette tapes. Once, I became intrigued with the artist's lyrics, particularly the reference to Bogie and Bacall. A quick search on my iPhone revealed the song to be "Key Largo " by Bertie Higgins. The internal workings of the mind amaze me, because Bertie Higgins's lyrics created the idea of renting old Bogart movies on Netflix. Lexie and I started with *Casablanca*, where we began romanticizing old Hollywood and the era where the likes of Humphrey Bogart and Audrey Hepburn seemed so cool in the way they took a drag off their cigarettes. So, Lexie and I would do our best imitations.

What is the cliché, "Old habits die hard"? To call my two-week smoking a hobby is a stretch, but I returned to the hobby again in early April of the pandemic year. It was a trip to the grocery store that broke the seal, where I bought a box of Marsh Wheeling cigars. My new inspiration was the Clint Eastwood Spaghetti Westerns I'd started watching in lieu of *NCIS*. I had time to kill now, so I began taking long four-mile hikes with Honey. I did my best to hide my new habit from Lana by waiting until I was a few miles away from her family home before I lit up a stogie.

Then it happened. I remember the day and conversation well. I had just packed two Marsh Wheelings in my front jean pocket and was in the process of attaching Honey's leash to her red collar when Lana appeared from the corner of the house. The cigars were already carefully tucked away, so I was not worried at all. As Lana approached Honey and I on the gray slate outdoor back porch, she asked, "Matty, would you and Honey mind if I joined you."

"No, that would be great."

Honey wagged her tail in excitement. Lana took Honey's leash from me, and we began walking through the rolling back fields of the estate toward the lake. Our typical hike entailed circling the lake four or five times and then proceeded to the woods before returning and making a few more laps.

As we started to near the three-foot blue flag iris plants with the bright purple flowers in full bloom, Lana asked, "Is this about the time when you have your cigar?"

I paused and searched.

"You know about that Lana?"

"Of course, I do."

"How?"

"Matty, it's thoughtful of you not to smoke in or near my parents' house, but I can still smell the cigars on your hands and honestly, the lake is not so far from the house. I can literally see you smoking them. Truth be told. The Marsh Wheeling shipments arriving at the house were a dead giveaway, too."

I did not know how to respond or what to say. Should I apologize? Did I do something wrong or offensive? I felt guilty for hiding the habit.

"Lana, I guess it's safe to assume you would like me to stop smoking cigars, right?"

"Matty, I am not going to tell you what to do. You may want to consider stopping not for me but rather for you. We both know what the long-term implications are, including emphysema, lung cancer, heart disease. I'm not painting the prettiest of pictures for you here, I know."

I knew she was right and at some point, I planned to stop. For my own good, the sooner I kicked the habit the better. What happened next absolutely shocked me. As I stood there with the cigar clenched between my pointer and middle finger, Lana carefully pried the cigar away from hand and slowly raised the cigar to her lips and took a drag. I had never seen Lana smoke anything.

"What's wrong Matty, you've never seen a woman smoke a cigar before?"

"Well, I cannot say that I have, but please take that with a grain of salt. I've never really seen anyone smoke a cigar aside from athletes on television after winning major championships. Have you smoked a cigar before?"

"Of course not, I never smoked anything, but that does not mean there cannot be a first time for me."

Her facial grimace at the taste of the cigar on her slightly chapped lips revealed her utter distaste with smoking. We continued our walk, passing the cigar back and forth.

After a silent while, Lana asked, "Matty, I definitely respect your right to privacy, but my parents are curious why you are not spending as much time with all of us as you initially did after dinner."

"Honestly, the only reason is that I can no longer stomach the news and your mom and dad seemed to be engulfed in learning every detail about COVID-19. All the negativity and finger pointing are just a bit much for me. I prefer the Cliff's Notes version of COVID-19 events which I can get by reading the internet. I really do not need hours on end and . . ."

I paused.

"And what Matty?"

"With my grandfather's recent death, I just do not want to be reminded of more deaths and the pain that people are suffering through. I had the opportunity to say goodbye before he left this earth. Most people in today's environment do not get the chance. Their loved ones end up in a hospital where no visitors are allowed and after they die, there is not even a funeral."

"I completely understand. I wish you would have just shared how you were feeling about the current situation. Is there something I can do to help?"

"Actually, yes, it's something that we can do together if you are not too tied up with your trial."

Lana's deep blue eyes opened widely. She answered, "I'm up for anything Matty. What do you have in mind?"

"Let's take some Georgia road trips over the next few months. That is if the national parks are open. I have walked through the concourse F at Atlanta Hartsfield Airport countless times, and I am always enamored of the photography which shows all that Georgia has to offer. From canyons and gorges, to waterfalls, there is all this beauty that can be reached within a four-hour drive and even though I have lived here over twenty years, I have never experienced any of these places."

Lana smiled and said, "You know what, neither have I. What specifically are you thinking?"

"Funny you should ask. Yesterday after dinner, I went downstairs and did some basic research. I would love to visit Providence Canyon, Tallulah Gorge, and Amicalola Falls."

"Deal. Let's go."

COVID SURPRISES

For multiple months I had successfully been able to distract myself from the thoughts and images of Lana kissing Jack. Then June arrived and the ultimate diversion surfaced. Eddie was fully aware of my pet peeve against texting but regardless he texted me the words, "please call me asap."

What was so urgent?

I will never forget the sound of his voice cracking as he began our conversation saying, "Matty, I . . ." His voice kept breaking.

"Matty, I have some very unexpected news for you."

My mind immediately gravitated to the thought of his aging grandparents or parents having contracted COVID. I began to fear the worse as I held on for his next sentence.

"Daisy is pregnant."

"Thank God."

"What?" answered Eddie.

"I immediately assumed the worst that someone in your family had COVID and was deathly ill. This is the news of life, not death."

"But Matty, Daisy and I are not married. We have not told anybody, and she is not sure if she wants to have the baby."

"I see. What is it that you want?"

"That's it Matty. I have no idea. You know how I feel about these things. I would prefer that she had the baby."

"Eddie, have you shared the way you feel with her?"

"Not yet. The news is only three weeks old, and we did not want to panic, but the doctor confirmed that this is no false alarm."

"Do you love Daisy?"

"Yes, of course I do. Why?"

"That is what matters most in the end. Does she love you?"

"Yes, she shared that she is very much in love with me."

"Then what is the problem?"

"Well, Matty, you know how religious my parents are. First, we are not even married, and second they would not approve of terminating the pregnancy."

"Eddie, this is about you and Daisy. Why don't you just tell her how you feel and that you want to have a baby with her?"

"Matty, you make it seem so easy. You do not see the difficulty in addressing the hippo in the room."

I laughed because Eddie always found a way to inject levity into profoundly serious conversations and I always appeased his tangents, at least temporarily, before returning to the main subject at hand.

"Eddie, I think you mean elephant in the room, right?"

"No, I think it is offensive to elephants to always use them as part of the analogy just based on their sheer size and weight."

"But you think it's appropriate to use the hippo metaphoric idiom."

"No, I think the word idiom sounds offensive though."

"Ok, let's put the topic of large zoo animals to the side. The fact is you are making the conversation with Daisy far too complicated. The easiest thing for you to do is to share your feelings with her. Be completely honest with what is in your heart."

"Thanks, Matty. I'll think about it."

"Anytime."

"I'll call you soon. I just need some time to think. By the way, Matty, I really miss our talks. It's just not the same as sitting together in the living room having this back-and-forth dialogue."

"Me too buddy, it's just not the same. Bye Eddie."

"Take care Matty."

I sat down at the office desk and leaned back in the netted Steelcase chair. I stared out the floor-to-ceiling window watching the soft breeze create small ripples on the dark blue pool water. My thoughts drifted to COVID, and I began thinking about a year in which many people would exit this world, while others would enter. How many people who passed away in the last four months would have ever thought that 2020 would be the last year of their life? Fathers, mothers, daughters, sons, brothers, and friends probably had no idea in 2019 that a once-in-a-hundred-year pandemic would arrive. Countless people had probably looked forward to the next year and the many milestones their families would be celebrating. No one in 2019 would have considered that their wedding, graduation, prom, or dream vacation would not be possible, or at least drastically different than they originally planned and anticipated.

Our lives are so fragile. Within a moment, everything can turn on a dime, forever changing the way we live, or lived, depending on the case. I imagined those that died of COVID. How differently would they have lived in 2019 knowing that 2020 would be the last year of their life? People constantly push things out, delaying their dreams, prolonging the time they need to forgive others, not saying three simple words like, *I love you*. I thought about the parents and grandparents who would miss their child's wedding, births, or celebrating their own anniversary.

On the other side of the tragedies of COVID are the new lives or milestones. Everyone will have their own COVID story. I started to recognize that I had the ability to shape my own COVID experience. Everyone who was living through this pandemic had the ability to determine how they would spend their time and whether the experience would result in a positive story or a negative one. We all get to write our own individual life narratives. Every decision we make results in part of our story, and it is the series of small stories that builds each individual chapter of our lives.

I thought about how I had wasted away the early days of lockdown by watching television or viewing the same movie that I had probably already seen a dozen times. What if in the next few months my life came to an end? How many regrets would I have as I laid in a hospital bed with no way to change the long-term outcome?

I spent the better part of an hour wrestling with the idea of forgiveness. Lana's trial was not scheduled until August after the courts delayed trials and shifted schedules. Although August was just four months away, it felt more like years for me.

When I first heard about Lana's criminal charge of insider trading, my top focus was on her innocence, but after learning about her and Jack, I began to recognize that I was growing less concerned about Lana and more concerned about me. I desperately desired to understand the details behind the kiss between Lana and Jack, and if indeed anything happened beyond just a kiss. But if I loved Lana with all my heart, regardless of what transpired between Jack and Lana, I would forgive, and my hope would be for her freedom. Even if we were to never get married, the single most important element of our relationship should be for me to stand by her. There is no downside to forgiveness, only upside.

Right?

INSIGNIFICANT ONE

The next morning, I woke up inspired at the thought of using the once in a lifetime pandemic as an opportunity to pursue an unrealized dream of mine. For years I had been toiling at the idea of writing my first novel, but for whatever reason I contrived, there was never any time. The excuses I had long used like fatigue from traveling, lack of downtime during the week, or busy weekends were no longer valid. Before sitting down at the desk in my future in-law's lavish basement office, I decided to go for a run to clear my head.

Honey and I set out for a long trek where I hoped to gain some insights into what I could base my novel on. Mile after mile passed, but then somewhere within the sixth mile, as I started towards the house, I was struck with a premise for the book. A surreal feeling overcame me as I hoped to capture each thought then entering my mind. I returned to a conversation that my friend David and I had about insignificant and consequential others. I decided that I would run with this theme.

As soon as I entered the house, I went directly to the long espresso-colored desk proceeding to remove my laptop from the drawer. Alongside the laptop was the copy of *The Sun Also Rises* and a picture of Skylar, both of which had been collecting dust for several months now. The revisiting of the Hemingway classic would be delayed indefinitely as I endeavored to begin my own author's journey. I propped the picture of Skylar and me up against a framed picture of Mackinac Island. The Trangates used pictures of their various vacations as home décor. I particularly was drawn to this one which featured the sun setting with sailboats tied to moors about fifty yards away while two empty white wooden Adirondack chairs sat onshore on a large flat grass-covered field. In the distance was a beautiful lighthouse that was catching the brilliant reflection of the setting sun.

I searched for the details that I never quite connected during my relationship with Skylar. She entered my life quite abruptly. At the time I met her, I had been in a yearlong relationship with a girl named Melissa. Melissa worked in the accounting department of the *New Atlanta Times*. We met in the nearly empty company cafeteria. Both of us had taken a late lunch and rather than sit alone in the large open-air café, we decided to sit together. A few months later we began dating, and the relationship was more than a year old when Skylar entered the picture.

There was nothing extraordinary about the relationship with Melissa. The most positive aspect of our time together was that there was no drama. Very rarely did the two of us disagree, and to the best I can recall we never had an argument. I imagine that if the relationship continued, I would have eventually proposed and proceeded on with life, settling down somewhere in the greater suburbs of Atlanta like Alpharetta. We would have elected to live somewhere like this because of the school districts. Melissa's personality was pleasant, and she had this girl-next-door likeability. I cannot imagine anyone disliking her.

Skylar entered my life unexpectedly. The newspaper was working with the graphic design firm that employed her, and they assigned me to be part of the team that interfaced with her firm on the new layout for the sports page. Most likely my boss assigned me to this role because he knew the other senior writers would be irritated by working on such a project. Her long flowing blond hair and deep blue Mediterranean eyes immediately attracted me. There was a mystique about her which to this day I find difficult to describe. Skylar's aura drew me in, and with each passing day my fascination with her grew. Despite the natural attraction, I never pursued Skylar. I remained loyal to Melissa up until the point when Skylar invited me to visit the Trois Gallery, which was displaying some of her work and the work of her fellow SCAD alumni and students.

I asked Melissa if she would be alright with me visiting the gallery with Skylar and she said yes. When the day of the exhibition arrived, I took the Marta from Buckhead to meet

Skylar. Up to that point, most of my cultural experiences stemmed from watching cartoons as a child. My image of an opera was based on the episode of Bugs Bunny where Bugs and Elmer Fudd performed. The main goal for me that evening was to not appear uncouth while I attempted to fake a minimal level of cultural sophistication.

I patiently waited for Skylar outside the gray façade building with a large sign which spelled out SCAD, Savannah College of Art and Design. There was never an occasion where Melissa was late, so when forty-five plus minutes had expired, I began to assume that Skylar would be a no-show. Just as I began to devise my plan B of leaving SCAD and catching a movie back in Buckhead, Skylar appeared. Her yellow locks swirled around her shoulders like a Hollywood starlet. Skylar donned stylish, black-rimmed Lisa Loeb glasses. Her eyewear complimented her violet dress. The short form-fitting purple dress included streaks of gray that traced her body and reminded me of straws with colorful swirls. Then to complete her ensemble she wore gray high heels with straps that crawled up her legs like Cleopatra's golden arm bands.

Clearly, Skylar was out of my league from many perspectives. Her wardrobe that evening was probably more expensive than every piece of clothing I owned. She carried herself with a level of grace, elegance, and refinement which far exceeded what I was capable of. Skylar took me by the arm as though I were an usher leading her down the red carpet of a Hollywood premier. Her friends loved praising both her artwork and style. I assumed that people took me to be an assistant of hers who hailed taxis, carried her bags, and scheduled her appointments. The night flew by and ended with a drink at the sleek W Hotel bar on 14th Street. This is when I discovered Skylar's penchant for martinis, which always had to be extra dry with three green olives.

That was a night of many firsts for me. I never drank a martini before, never attended an art gallery, and was never drawn to someone who was so indescribably mysterious and sophisticated. After a few drinks I realized that the attraction between us was mutual. Skylar tempted me to no end to return home with her, but I could not do that to Melissa. I remained loyal the entire evening and would not betray my girlfriend. At the same time, I realized that the relationship with Melissa would soon end, and it would be because of my decision.

I was in no condition to take the Marta back to Buckhead, so I hailed a taxi. Skylar texted me through my cab ride back to the Eclipse attempting to convince me to return to her midtown apartment. I felt like a sailor sailing between the Scylla and the Charybdis as I kept fighting the temptation to return to midtown, where the six-headed monster waited on one side of the strait, the swirling whirlpool on the other.

The next week I felt as though I was walking on eggshells with Melissa because I knew I had to end the relationship with her, but at the same time, I did not want to hurt her. When the time finally arrived to have the adult conversation that I had been avoiding, it went much smoother than I thought. Melissa met me at Eddie's condo and took a seat on my bed as I nervously paced about the room. She graciously introduced the break-up topic sensing that we were needing to have an honest but extremely difficult conversation. Tears trickled down her cheeks while my heart sank watching her absorb the news. I never ended a relationship in this way before where I was breaking up with one person to pursue another. All my previous relationships ended in different ways. On several occasions I was in the same position as Melissa. I could empathize with how she must have felt. Those situations always sting, and the longer the relationship that preceded the break-up, the deeper the hurt and the longer the recovery would take.

My sincere hope was that Melissa's heart was scarred but not broken and that she would soon meet someone more compatible with her than I ever was.

But my heart was with Skylar. We started seeing each other about a week after my relationship with Melissa ended. Skylar was unlike anyone I ever dated. How our orbits came together and ultimately collided is unbeknownst to me. She could have easily just been the artistic graphic designer that I knew as a casual acquaintance through work, but fate took the two of us on a separate journey. Skylar touched my soul in a distinct way, taking me to the depths of understanding myself. She challenged me to go beyond my conventional way of thinking. Her modus operandi was to explore deeply personal questions which required extensive thought. Skylar had a raspy voice which greatly contrasted with her soft delicate laugh.

One conversation that comes to mind is when she challenged me to describe my definition of the meaning of life. I can still picture her sitting with legs crossed on the soft powder blue ottoman in her apartment. She had just finished playing a new song for me on her acoustic guitar, which was now resting against her light-green suede sofa. "Tell me something Matty?"

"What would you like me to tell you?"

"Describe what you believe the meaning of life to be?"

"Seriously?"

"Yes Matty, seriously, and I want to know the details."

I sighed, lifting my café latte as I attempted to search for an answer that would suffice. I then proceeded into a rather long monologue along the lines of, "All right. You want me to describe what I perceive the meaning of life to be."

"That's right. Go."

"I am going to approach this from a non-spiritual point of view. Okay?"

"Fine."

"I suppose we need to start with when our lives begin. If we use birth as the genesis of our individual lives, then our birth is the foundation upon which everything centers on. An infant or newborn enters the world in a perfect state. A child that has just entered the world is completely perfect and innocent. Are you following me?"

Skylar smiled and said, "Yes, your every word."

"Well, that child is completely dependent on someone else for everything. The child needs someone to feed them, to clothe them for warmth, to change them after a biological release, and to be loved. Based on needing something for every vital aspect of their life, they develop indisputable trust. The child cannot fail anyone because they are not yet capable of doing anything for themselves. Right?"

Skylar shifted a bit on the ottoman.

"Okay Matty, I'm with you on the child, but what is the link to my original question on the meaning of life?"

"Patience, Skylar. I'm getting there. Because the child is one hundred percent trusting and incapable of even the simplest of tasks, they retain their perfect state over a period. During this time, think about how they cannot speak either. This child has never hurt anyone or lied to anyone because they are not yet capable of doing so."

Skylar smiled and with her raspy voice, said, "I'm starting to see where you are going with this."

"As the child grows and becomes more independent, they become imperfect overtime. As they progress through their childhood, they will eventually say hurtful things, act in angry or aggressive ways, speak dishonestly, and lose trust. Over time from childhood to adolescence then eventually adulthood, the person becomes even more imperfect, which ultimately brings me to the meaning of life. At least what I perceive today at this exact time to be the meaning of life.

"The meaning of life is to minimize our level of imperfection. No single person will ever be perfect. That is beyond the realm of possibility. We all want the opportunity to be less imperfect."

"How is that?" asked Skylar.

"Simple. The more honest we are, the less hurtful we are, and the more forgiving we are. These are all ways of being less imperfect. Think about spending the last days of your life and how you would like to be remembered. Everyone has the potential to be friendly and kind. Tiny behaviors that result in a smile or simple thank you can make the largest impact on both the people we know personally and the complete strangers or passersby whose lives intersect with ours, if ever so briefly. Smiling and laughing are far better alternatives than frowning and moping. Choosing to be friendly is much more appealing than electing to be mean. Saying hello even to a stranger is much nicer than completely ignoring someone."

"If I understand you correctly, you equate the meaning of life to being a good or pleasant person."

"Yes, but at a much deeper level than being friendly or kind."

"How so?"

I knew I had intrigued Skylar at this point. "Anyone can project a friendly exterior, and in their own clever ways, people can fake cordiality. The more challenging proposition is yielding or putting others ahead of oneself by being honest, faithful, forgiving, and loving. Someone who truly places the needs of others in front of their own is striving toward what I would call being less imperfect. Being less imperfect is the true measure of living up to the meaning of life. There's an old saying that everybody dies but not everybody lives. Life is defined by merely existing, but living a great life cannot be merely defined by existing. A great life is defined by your contribution to humanity, and not tangible contributions, because those are easily forgotten."

"So, you are saying that those who cure a disease, or create an artistic timepiece, or invent technology that changes humanity, are less important than kindness."

"What I'm saying, Skylar, is that contributions come in many forms, but for most people their tangible contributions are easily forgotten while the intangible can last through multiple generations. Take some modern-day examples like Mark Zuckerberg, Steve Jobs, and Bill Gates. These people will be remembered throughout history because of their contributions, namely Facebook, Microsoft, and Apple and the products or services associated with those companies. Do you know all three of these people?"

"Yes, of course."

I continued, "Can you tell me who developed the idea for the Like feature on Facebook, or designed the pivot table feature into Excel, or Facetime application?"

She shook her head. "You see, these were significant contributions that billions of people use on a daily basis, but few people know who actually worked on these products within their respective companies."

Skylar stopped me and pulled me onto the couch where we embraced. This type of back-and-forth dialogue occurred regularly and was unlike any emotional relationship that I had ever experienced before. Our relationship started in September and with each passing week I had no idea of where our romance was headed. Unlike other girls I dated, there was no discussion of a future together. We lived by the moment, which was exciting and terrifying at the same time. The bond between us always seemed a bit shaky or unstable like an anchor that drifted along the sea of the ocean floor with the wind instead of holding in place.

A knock at the door interrupted my reverie, followed by the sound of Lana's voice.

"Matty, are you in there, can I come in?"

"Yes, of course."

Lana entered the room in a two-piece bikini with yellow and blue alternating vertical stripes. She looked amazing.

"Matty, would like to join me for a swim?"

"I would love to."

She walked over to the desk where I was writing my novel and spun my chair back around facing my laptop and monitor. She kissed me on the back of the neck. "What are you working on?"

I rotated the chair one hundred eighty degrees so that I could look into her deep dark eyes. I pulled her on top of me and kissed her until Lana pulled away.

"I'm sorry Matty, but my mom is outside doing yoga." She paused. "Who is that a picture of?"

Without having to turn around I knew that the picture of Skylar was still leaning against her parents framed Mackinac Island photo.

"That's Skylar. The relationship I had with her is the basis for my debut novel. That is what I was working on before you came downstairs."

Lana's facial expression looked like a combination of being puzzled and concerned.

"Should I be concerned that the central character in your first novel is an ex-girlfriend?"

I detested any conflict with Lana that may escalate into an argument. Given the fragile nature of our relationship going back to when I learned about the kiss between her and Jack, concern started to build up inside me. Prior to the Jack conflict we only entered disputes on the rarest of occasions. Lana won most of our arguments and many times I discovered in the middle of the conflict that she was right, and I was wrong. Coming to understand that I was incorrect was never the issue. Admitting that to Lana is what required humility. How could I reduce the intensity of Lana's concern about my novel? Only complete honesty and transparency would suffice.

I took Lana by both hands, looking deeply into her eyes.

"Lana, you should not be concerned about Skylar. Skylar is a character in the book but not one of the main characters. Please give me the time to explain. I never shared the details of my relationship with Skylar with you. You know about my previous relationships with Lexie and Melissa because the ending of those was easier and lighter to explain. Those relationships ran their course and concluded in a mutually cordial way."

Lana stopped me. "Matty, what is so special or defining about the relationship you had with Skylar, and what is it that you are protecting her from or me from?"

I took a breath. "Until recently I could never understand the complexity surrounding the relationship Skylar and I had, at least not in any way that I could articulate. That is until recently when David explained the concept of an insignificant one and how consequential the person's role was in our lives. Then everything began to make sense."

"What is the concept of an insignificant one or consequential others?"

"Lana, I never met anyone like Skylar before. She was pretty, mysterious, artistic, and challenged me to think beyond my way of thinking. Somehow, she tapped into my soul in a way no one had before. Our connection resonated deeply inside me.

"Skylar was anything but conventional. She asked profoundly personal questions to the point of being intrusive. Skylar dressed in a way that set herself apart from others. She drove an old 1970s light blue four-door diesel convertible Volvo that she filled with her own blends of biodiesel using leftover food products from a local Decatur restaurant. She reminded me of a brilliant movie star from the 1960s in not only her behavior but also her innate beauty. Skylar even had a distinct smell. She wore patchouli oil."

"Matty, was your attraction to Skylar or to the way you romanticized her?"

She had a point about my tendency to romanticize certain aspects of life. In my twenties I often painted a picture of how I perceived life would be instead of how it was. Starting in my mid-thirties I started seeing life differently. The first time I covered the Padres, I fell in love with the quaint beach towns north of the city. A friend of mine from college lived in Encinitas and showed me around the area. I immediately fell in love, imagining a future life in Solana Beach where I would surf every day and eat fish tacos at the locally owned restaurants on the coast. I struggled to separate fact from fiction. In fact, I surfed on only a few occasions before this and I could get up on the board, but my skills were nothing like the image I created of my future self where I would live in the small sleepy beach towns along the bluff.

Nowadays the Southern California dream and lifestyle that I long sought have crashed like waves crashing on a rocky beach. The romanticized ideas ended because I realized their impracticality. I could not afford to live in that part of the country, never mind my dreams of being a proficient surfer. I much prefer swimming in the warm waters of the Gulf of Mexico to the frigid Pacific Ocean. Besides, I still get the benefit of experiencing the beauty of Southern California every time the Braves have an away series with the Padres. I always find a way to spend a morning in Encinitas where I grab breakfast at the Potato Shack or stop by Las Olas in Cardiff-by-the-Sea for grilled fish tacos and a margarita. A visit or two a year to these local paradises suffice for my small sleepy beach town fix.

Lana struck a chord because I was in my mid-twenties when Skylar and I dated. Ten years ago, I would have most certainly portrayed my relationship with Skylar in a cinematic way. The same can probably be said about the relationships with Lexie and Melissa. Perspective and wisdom come from life experience. The idealistic concepts that were part of my thinking a decade ago have been displaced with more optimistic realism. I recognize that life is not a Disney movie or a

Hollywood romantic comedy where poor twenty-somethings live in million-dollar flats off Central Park. That perfect Sunday morning brunch lifestyle and idealism all came together in the way I perceived Skylar.

Lana patiently awaited my response. "You are right. I probably romanticized my relationship with Skylar."

"What are you not telling Matty?"

This would be the first time that I went into any detail with anyone about my relationship with Skylar. As I prepared to explain everything to Lana, I recognized for the first time that I was not protecting Skylar all these years but rather myself. I concealed the wounds and scars on my heart all this time, not giving them oxygen, they needed to heal. Now, sitting before Lana, time seemed frozen.

"Buckle up Lana. I have never shared any of this information with anyone. First, I should begin with the length of our relationship. Skylar and I only dated for six months, which I know seems short. Like most new relationships, ours was exciting in the earliest few months as we bonded and discovered new things about each other every day. Skylar introduced me to a bonanza of first-time cultural experiences. In less than three months' time, I went to an art gallery exhibit, attended the opera at the Fox, and participated in a poetry reading. Life with her in those early days was thrilling and terrifying because I was living a life way outside of my comfort zone. There were so many firsts."

I knew exactly how to answer this because the premise of my novel would be based on the answer to this very question.

"Lana, that is the point. What is just as important as to the how and why the relationship with Skylar ended is how we came together to be a couple. The answer to this question is the core of the insignificant or consequential principle. You see, I broke up with Melissa in order to go out with Skylar. The breakup is the first key pillar to the principle. The second pillar is how the relationship ended. You are right. Skylar was a free spirit, perhaps the freest of spirits. We had been together for about five months when things started to unravel. Skylar started traveling to Portland, Oregon; well, not Portland but Beaverton, Oregon. Her company staffed her on a project with Nike. I had a suspicion that she started cheating on me, which proved to be true. Skylar fell in love with what I like to call a shoe boy. I don't recall the guy's name, but he worked in the design department."

"And?" asked Lana.

"An insignificant other is a person that enters your life for a noticeably short period of time, but in that period they can make the largest impact on your future life without ever knowing. If my universe and Skylar's never intersected, I would have probably continued to date Melissa and potentially married her. Melissa and I were perfectly compatible and the normal life trajectory of a happy couple that proceeds to engagement then marriage. I took a major risk in pursuing Skylar. The fallout with Skylar ultimately led me to you. Skylar is my insignificant other that connected me with my significant other. She's a throwaway character in a novel that plays a small but pivotal role, but far from the leading part. You will be cast as the main character in not only my novel but most importantly my life. I love you, Lana."

Lana grinned and appeared to be digesting the principle I explained. Her legalistic brain seemed to be firing on all cylinders, digesting the data and synthesizing everything into a clear and concise form.

She pulled me close.

"I love you too. The funny thing is that I too have an insignificant other, but I guess you already surmised that. Assuming I look at my life through the same contextual analysis you have, Jack is that person. Who knows? Maybe I needed to experience a jerk before I met you so that I could fully appreciate you."

"Lana, I sense that you still question the premise of principle?"

"Matty, what I am about to tell you may not be so obvious to you. Your explanation of what drew you close to Skylar mainly centered on your physical attraction to her and this aura she had. The attributes of how she touched your soul through her mystical appeal were already present inside you. Those were your thoughts, ideas, and mindset—not hers. In fact, you never touched upon her own brilliance or intellectual prowess."

What Lana revealed never occurred to me. Was she right that I created a grandiose version of Skylar in my mind?

"Lana, what are you getting at?"

"You see Matty, you put Skylar on this pedestal where she has remained for all these years, untouched by everyone, including you. What did she do to deserve that status?"

"I never considered that."

"The main difference between our insignificant ones or others is that I understood and clearly saw Jack's flaws. Surely, Skylar was not as perfect as you made her out to be. Of course, I do not know her, and you have the misfortune of knowing Jack, so if I asked you about Jack's shortcomings, how would you answer?"

"I would say arrogance, pride, and lack of empathy."

"Thank you Matty for proving my point. Those flaws are how I would answer the same question and if I knew Skylar, I could probably point out some of her personal weaknesses as well. None of us are perfect Matty, not you and certainly not me."

"You're right."

"This is not a right or wrong conversation. Matty, what I love about you most is that you have the external optimism of a child unlike any other person I know. Most adults become jaded or cynical over time with each passing disappointment or heart break but not you. I love you Matty, more than I can possibly express to you. Let's find a way to get away for a while. Just the two of us."

Of course, I agreed. Lana achieved in the span of an hour what I failed to do over the course of five years. She removed the blinders. Skylar was much more than an insignificant other, she was a fictional character I created that placed her above everyone else. For the next several days, I thought about all the time and energy invested into thinking that Skylar was more than she really was.

Skylar played a minor role in a transitional season of my life. As I continued to think about her and wrote additional chapters in my novel, I discovered that the aspects of her that initially attracted me to her the most would detract me from someone like her today. The cultural appeal of attending an opera or going to a gallery exhibit were now of no interest to me. I would prefer to have dinner at a local eatery or catch a new acoustic act. I have a much better understanding of who I am now and who I am not. My days of living out a cinematic version of life have passed by with no signs of returning.

LOCKED OUTSIDE

Lana's suggestion of some time away made a lot of sense. The locked-inside nature of the pandemic eventually created a stir-crazy feeling, which I desperately needed to escape. Ever since I was a kid, I loathed spending hours upon hours indoors. Embracing the seasonal climate fluctuations that occur in the northeast, my brothers and I transitioned from one season's outdoor activities to the next. We played pick-up sports year-round, rotating from tackle football in our next-door neighbor's backyard in the fall to soccer in the spring and baseball in the summer. There were times as a kid growing up where I found myself locked outside of my parents' house. And it really didn't matter, if there was a ball nearby and if I was wearing the proper clothing.

With COVID-19 and the extensive lockdowns I embraced the concept of being locked *outside*. So, when Lana agreed to take an overnight road trip with me, and the Trangates agreed to take care of Honey for a few days, I jumped at the opportunity. We departed Milton, Georgia, late Friday afternoon. Lana cautioned me more than once to watch my speed as we drove southbound on Interstate 85. I pushed the limits of my Toyota Prius, racing time with the intention of arriving at Providence Canyon before sunset. Lana turned up the radio when John Mayer started singing "Why Georgia" on Sirius Coffeehouse. One of many magical experiences of an extended drive with a fellow passenger occurs when you discover something new about them.

Lana shocked me with her John Mayer story. Despite the length of our three-year-long relationship, she never divulged having met the famous musician. Lana explained the context of Georgia in the early 2000s when John was writing and releasing his debut album, *Room for Squares*. At the time, she didn't know John Mayer from John Smoltz. They both were attending a Georgia Tech party where their paths crossed, and they introduced themselves. Lana had absolutely no idea that John Mayer was a rising star until a few moments later when a friend of hers asked her if she knew who she had just spoken to. Lana casually answered, "Yes, that's John."

"John Mayer, right?"

"I don't know, it's John from Atlanta."

Lana later discovered from her friend that John Mayer was becoming a famous musician and would soon start a national tour. Lana's story reminded me of how pure her heart is and that regardless of who the person is, everyone should be treated with respect and dignity. I doubt Lana would have acted any differently had she known that she was speaking to a future multi-Grammy award winner.

We arrived at Providence Canyon State Park just as the sun began to descend. Huge tall Georgia pines spanned the distance across the horizon while the yellow rays of the setting sun lit up the canyon walls with brilliant reds and oranges. We stood at the top of the canyon watching the sun dip below the horizon. The depth of the canyon became even more impressive as the sunlight faded. Lana and I waited to leave until the sun disappeared then drove to the Marriott in Columbus, Georgia. This would be the first time we had not slept in her parent's home in Milton since the pandemic. Checking into the hotel caused an eerie feeling in the pit of my stomach. I felt as though I was doing something wrong, despite having spent hundreds upon hundreds of evenings in Marriott hotels over the past eight years.

We proceeded to drop off our bags in the room, then back downstairs to the bar of the Houlihan's located in the hotel. Everything seemed surreal, as though we had escaped from prison to get a glimpse of what life had been like before the pandemic. Despite our best attempts, neither of us felt completely at ease. Both of us practiced all the COVID guidelines but being in a hotel for the first time since the lockdown and sitting down at a bar seemed like a guilty pleasure. A man in his late fifties started to put us at ease. I did not catch his name but learned that he was in the process of completing a cross-country motorcycle trip. The gray-haired man with a neatly trimmed goatee lived in Sanibel, Florida.

Lana and I vacationed in Sanibel a few years prior, so we had an idea of what life in retirement was like there. I imagined waking up and taking long morning walks along the shore collecting the seashells before riding our bicycles to the Over Easy Café for breakfast. After breakfast we would return home to read or write for a few hours then spend some time at the beach. Our days would end watching the sun fall into the Gulf of Mexico.

The kind man explained how he left Florida several months before and that his wife had been waiting for him to return. He described his wife as more of a home body with an aversion to riding motorcycles. Somehow, we stumbled upon the topic of triathlons and the retired Floridian went into more detail of his past life. Lana and I were impressed with the gentleman's athletic prowess. Both the man and his first wife competed in ironman triathlons. I sensed that these were triumphant yet sad times for him. He referenced the time the two of them invested in training began to unravel their marriage. We finished our dinner wishing the man a safe return to Sanibel then headed up to our room.

I woke up early the next morning before Lana. I quietly left the room to go for a run. The hotel was quiet except for a few people sitting in the lobby having their morning coffee. The fiberglass sheet that separated the hotel clerk from the guests at the front desk served as a constant reminder of the once in a hundred-year pandemic. I removed my mask and placed it in the Prius before I set out to run along the shores of the Chattahoochee River. Only a few people walked along the Riverwalk that hugged the banks of the river. I felt liberated running along the swiftly flowing waterway. The old industrial brick buildings along the banks had been recently repurposed into condos and lofts. I thought back to their former purpose of producing goods that would be loaded on vessels and transported up and down the river.

My run started north for a few miles before turning around at the construction site of a new hospital. I headed south back towards the Marriott but took a slight detour running west across the brick-lined 14th Street Pedestrian Bridge into Alabama. The long run provided me with time to organize my thoughts and for deep reflection. Lana and I were successfully working through our relationship challenges, and within several weeks her trial would begin. The two of us came a long way over the past six months. I cannot say if the pandemic helped to save our relationship or not. COVID-19 certainly put us in a better position to resolve the hurdles we faced. The time on my Timex indicated I had been running for over an hour. I loved the feeling of being locked outside that morning but needed to return to the hotel to have breakfast with my beautiful fiancée before returning to hike down Providence Canyon.

THE TRUTH UNFOLDS

The digital red neon lights of the vintage General Electric alarm clock radio blinked. Unease built up inside me as I watched the minute reading on the display tick up. Sometime after 2 AM I fell into an exceptionally light sleep. It was a Sunday in early July, the day before the first day of Lana's trial. Our future hung in the balance. Would she be convicted of this crime?

After a shower and shave, I joined Lana and her family upstairs before breakfast. I opened the screen door to let Honey outside and was immediately hit by the hot humid southern summer. Once she'd returned, I proceeded upstairs for breakfast, where the setting was more jovial than I anticipated. I wrongly assumed that everyone would be anxious and quiet. But Mr. Trangate walked over to the coffee maker for the half full pot to refresh everyone's cup.

"Thank you, Angelo," said Mrs. Trangate.

"You're welcome, Lena."

The breakfast nook overlooked the pool area and the woods beyond. Mr. and Mrs. Trangate sat at opposite ends of the light pine kitchen table. Two long benches provided additional seating for six on opposite sides of the table. Throughout the pandemic, Lana and I sat in the middle of the benches across from one another. Lana quietly ate her egg whites and wheat toast, smiling as Lena led most of the morning conversation. She looked at ease and displayed no sign of fear or anxiety. Her calm demeanor amazed me.

"How did you sleep, Matty?" asked Mrs. Trangate.

I sensed that Lana and her parents all knew the answer to the question.

"Truthfully, I slept terribly."

Lana smiled at me before lifting her light blue coffee mug to her lips. Then she looked down at her watch before excusing herself, walking her plate to the large white farm sink, and saying goodbye.

After breakfast, I returned downstairs to write an article for an upcoming deadline. The season was scheduled to commence on July 23, with sixty games scheduled through September, followed by a sixteen-team playoff and the World Series in October. I struggled all morning to write a quality piece but eventually finished something acceptable and submitted it before noon.

I'd never written with a mock trial running through my mind. I had no sense of judicial proceedings other than the few episodes of *Bull* I watched with the Trangates during the pandemic. Lana provided us with no timetable on how long the trial would run. Selfishly, I hoped the duration would be days rather than weeks. Over the next few days, we didn't discuss the courtroom at all. Because of the pandemic and COVID procedures, we were unable to attend or even be present outside the courthouse. And I failed despite numerous attempts to gauge how the proceedings were moving. Lana gave neither positive nor negative indications of what she perceived the outcome to be. Friday arrived with no decision yet or news from Lana.

Week two moved quickly, with jury deliberations begun on Tuesday. Thursday the jury delivered their decision. I would have never predicted the outcome and my tangential involvement in the case. I felt naïve about not knowing anything and not questioning Lana more intensely. The iPhone sitting alongside my Mac started vibrating. I lifted the phone, reading Lana's name on the glass display. The next thing I heard was joy in her voice.

"Matty, it's all over. I was acquitted."

The news left me speechless. No insider trading. No fraud, shame, and prison time. "That's great, Lana. I'm so relieved."

Maybe she heard some hesitation in my voice because she started to explain the entire situation.

Raj and Kim suspected that Jack had been relaying confidential information on mergers and acquisitions that the firm was advising on to friends of his. Their suspicions grew, which led them to the FBI. Lana was more than willing to support the investigation, agreeing to work undercover on several M&A projects with Jack. Jack began to trust Lana and included her in the scheme. In exchange for providing confidential information to two of his investment banker friends from Duke, they paid him and Lana ten percent of the value of deals. The two Duke-grad bankers made over two million dollars in profit, while Jack and Lana were paid several hundred thousand dollars apiece.

The kiss occurred late one evening at a bar. Lana had worn a wire the entire day. Earlier in the day, Jack and Lana exchanged confidential information to the bankers, which in turn led to a wire transfer of funds to a Cayman Island-based bank account. This was the key evidence used in convicting Jack. For the first time, there was proof, both through wire-taped conversations and financial transactions, that Jack was committing fraud.

Jack invited Lana to have drinks after work to celebrate their newly minted financial success. Lana had no reason to believe Jack would pursue her because he was *happily married* with one young child and another on the way. After consuming a few too many drinks, he drunkenly attempted to woo Lana, kissing her lips and propositioning her to celebrate with him at an apartment he kept in downtown Atlanta. Lana broke the kiss and separated herself from Jack, reminding him that she was engaged, and that he is married.

"Lana, I'm so sorry that I thought you had cheated on me with Jack, but why didn't you tell me the details right away?"

"I couldn't, Matty."

"Why not?"

"Because the entire context of why I was with him that night could not be separated from the undercover operation. If I simply shared that I went out with Jack after work to celebrate and that it led to a kiss, you would have suspected something even deeper. It might have blown the whole thing. I'm so sorry to have involved you in this at all. Thank you for forgiving me. I know you wrestled with this for months, which was completely unfair. But now you see."

"Lana, I get it now and everything makes sense. You also indicated that I was tangentially involved though. How?"

"Do you remember the firm event we attended at the Georgian Terrace?"

"Yes of course."

"Do you recall a conversation with Raj and Kim about Fred Rogers?"

"Now that you mention it, yes, but what does Mr. Rogers have to do with any of this?"

"Matty, Raj and Kim were testing both of us. The name of the undercover operation was Fred Rogers. That was the genesis of working to catch Jack. When I stepped away that evening, the FBI put a wire on me so that I could begin trying to trap Jack. Raj and Kim needed to know that I did not share anything with you about the operation. The FBI was involved which required secrecy and *need to know* information. When you started talking about *Mr. Roger's Neighborhood*, in detail mind you, they knew that I never shared anything with you."

"How did they know that I wasn't just answering in the way I did to protect you."

"Matty, Raj and Kim are exceptionally talented lawyers. They know how to read people. In fact, they probably were analyzing you during your entire conversation with them. On a side note, Raj and Kim later commented to me about how great a guy you were. On that evening, they experienced your pure heart."

Questions continued to compile in my mind that I never anticipated. As the truth unfolded before me, my heart began to sink. My thoughts turned to Jack's young family, which included a wife, young daughter, and son.

"Lana, what happens next with Jack?"

"He will go to prison for eighteen months and be disbarred."

"What happens to his family then?"

"What do you mean?"

"He has a wife and two young kids. It seems like they are being punished as much as him."

"Matty, I would suspect that they would look to her parents or his for support while he is in prison."

Jack's sentence seemed just, but I could not escape the idea that his wife and children would be suffering at the expense of his poor life decisions. The consequences of his actions would alter the trajectory of their lives. Clearly, events and circumstances similar or even worse play out like this daily. Justice may always prevail, but the prevailing impact extends well beyond the guilty and accused.

At least one innocent person—my person—did the right thing. Lana and I celebrated her bravery that evening at 7 Acre BarnGrill. Ever since we relocated to her parents' house to quarantine in Milton, we fell in love with the quaint farm-to-table restaurant converted from an old General Store. The red wooden exterior with a silver roof created a rural modern welcome and the food was outstanding. Rather than wait for a table, we decided to have a standing dinner. We found a spot and stood adjacent to one another on opposing sides of the tall wooden barrel. I felt alive again. We could put the trial behind us. The start of the Major League Baseball season was coming.

Normally, I looked forward to hitting the road to cover the Braves, but this year I was happy to report on them remotely using Zoom. The COVID travel restrictions and MLB safety guidelines provided me with the opportunity to spend more time with Lana. After our nine-month roller coaster ride, which included not only her undercover operation but also the death of my grandfather, I looked forward to sailing on calmer waters.

With the wind at my back now, I felt free.

SAD FAMILIAR VOICE

Lana and I walked along the edge of the lake near the Trangates' home with Honey in tow when my phone started ringing. The last time Eddie and I spoke I learned that he and Daisy were excited about having a new baby. Baby Mia, named after Daisy's soccer star role model, Mia Hamm, would be entering the world sometime in December. Eddie shared the exact day with me, but the date never registered in my mind. After excusing myself from Lana and handing Honey's leash to her, I took Eddie's call.

I immediately stopped walking and motioned to Lana to continue without me. Eddie's voice broke as he relayed the sad news. Daisy miscarried two days prior. I struggled for the right words. "I'm sorry. Is there anything I can do?"

My question was met with gentle sobs and a sniffle.

Eddie shared some additional details about the day of this miscarriage. Daisy felt ill and rushed to the bathroom shortly after she woke up on Sunday morning. She fell to her knees on the cool bathroom tile floor and cried as she rested her arms on the closed lid of the toilet seat. Eddie joined her in the bathroom where he too wept. The two of them spent hours sobbing in the bathroom attempting to comfort one another. Eddie described the day as the worst day of his life.

The two of them had already started the conversion of my former room into a nursery. They ordered pink paint to match the light-gray crib that was on order from Pottery Barn. Daisy began registering items for her future baby shower. Then their hopes and dreams for a future with Mia were shattered.

Despite Eddie's earlier concerns, his parents had embraced the arrival of their future granddaughter. They never pressed him on not being married, rather emphasizing that he needed to put all his energy into supporting Daisy through her pregnancy. Daisy's parents too were thrilled at having their first granddaughter. My heart hurt for Eddie, who thanked me for listening and asked if we could speak again in a few days.

I could see Lana and Honey in the distance. They were at least a half mile away from me. Emotion overcame me while I stood there with the phone in my hand. Normally, I would wipe the tears away, but I just let them flow like the tide washing away the rough sand and seashells lying on the beach. Who could have predicted the type of year 2020 would turn out to be? Never in a single year had I experienced so many highs and lows. Pandemic aside, being on the brink of ending my engagement to Lana, recovering from the loss of my grandfather only a few months prior, experiencing a rebirth of my relationship with Lana, her acquittal, and now the loss of Daisy and Eddie's baby.

It was a lot for everybody.

Exhaustion and fatigue do not even begin to describe the way I felt. Then I thought too how fortunate I was. I had yet to experience the unexpected loss of a loved one from COVID-19, my employment remained steady, I had an extremely nice place to quarantine, including daily home cooked meals. No matter what my present circumstances were, someone else was living through a more difficult situation than I was. Just as I was about to start running my phone rang again. I lifted the phone seeing Eddie's name on the display.

"Hi Eddie."

"Hello Matty, hey, I hate to bother you again, but I need to ask you a huge favor."

"You're not bothering me. What can I do?"

"Daisy is going to spend a week with her parents, and I need to get away. Would you be able to take a trip with me?"

"Of course, I am ready to leave whenever you are. Where are we headed?"

"I was thinking about the Ft. Lauderdale and Pompano Beach area. I figure we are both working remotely so we just need a reliable high-speed internet connection. What do you think?"

"I'm in. Are you thinking about flying or driving?"

"Not flying with COVID. I was hoping we could drive down there along the Atlantic coast, taking breaks at small beach towns as we drove further south."

"Ok, sounds good. Do you want me to drive, or do you prefer to?"

"It would be great if you do not mind driving. I have been wanting to visit Pompano Beach ever since a friend gave me some investment advice, suggesting that I consider potential investment opportunities there."

"Eddie, I just need to ask Lana to take care of Honey while we are gone. When were you thinking about leaving?"

"I would love to leave as soon as possible."

"Ok Eddie, sounds good."

After Eddie and I concluded our call, I ran to catch up with Lana and Honey. She dropped Honey's leash and embraced me as I broke the news. I could feel her warm tears against my cheek. Ever since the pandemic and her acquittal, she never shared the depth of how she was feeling. I imagine the weight of all the events of 2020 fell upon Lana at once. I wished she could accompany me on the trip to Florida with Eddie.

BEACH BOUND

The day we were scheduled to depart, Eddie greeted me outside the front entrance of the Eclipse. I pushed on the hazard blinkers as he walked to the rear of the car to open the hatch for his suitcase. This was the first time I had seen Eddie in four months. He looked like a shell of his former self, with a slimmer build and long dark beard. This was the first time I ever saw him with facial hair. He looked completely drained and barely said a word. I pulled away as soon as the directions appeared on the heads-up display.

The deafening silence persisted for several hours. I would have preferred to listen to music, but Eddie had fallen asleep about an hour into the drive and the last thing on earth I wanted to do was disturb him. Who knew the last time he'd had a good sleep?

Eddie woke up just north of Macon asking where we were. He suggested we stop for the night, but he preferred to stay in a beach town instead of in the middle of north-central Florida. I stopped to get coffee at McDonald's and find a place to stay on the Atlantic coast in northern Florida. The Ritz Carlton on Amelia Island sounded about right, so I called to book a room. Eddie hardly responded to our new destination. Back on the road, I turned on some music. Soon, Eddie was back asleep.

While Eddie slumbered, I switched between satellite radio stations and took a kind of musical flux capacitor. Specific songs have this way of transporting me to different years, seasons, and life events. The Lemonheads' "It's a Shame About Ray" placed me back in high school where I was a seventeen-year-old kid driving my parents light-blue four door Oldsmobile 88. The V6 accelerated like a rocket, or at least I thought. The Lemonheads had such a great autumn sound.

We were just south of Brunswick when Eddie woke up and spotted the exit sign for Jekyll Island.

"Matty, can you get off at Jekyll Island for something to eat?"

I preferred to keep driving south but Eddie insisted we stop at The Wharf, a waterfront spot at the end of the long wooden boardwalk pier. Despite the hot and humid Georgia summer heat, we opted to sit outside on the deck at an open high-top bar. We listened to the acoustic guitarist play Jack Johnson covers as we waited for our drink orders. Katie Bender, the young singer-songwriter, mixed in her own brilliant songs, alternating between cover and her stuff.

As the late afternoon wore on, I noticed Eddie barely touched his Jekyll Boil, save for a shrimp or two. Eddie seemingly drank his dinner, ordering one wheat beer after another. I failed to notice how many glasses of Moon River Wild Wacky Wit he consumed. I hoped to arrive at the hotel before sunset, so I glanced down at my watch indicating to Eddie that we needed to get on the road. Eddie insisted on paying and leaned his weight on me as we walked back down the wooden pier slates toward the car. Within twenty minutes he fell asleep for the third time of the day—this time, passed out.

I drove in silence for the next hour and half until we arrived at the Ritz. Upon our arrival Eddie inquired about upgrading to a suite. He put all the charges on his credit card and handed me both room keys. I could not believe he agreed to pay so much for one night. 'Incredible' understates the expansive view of our suite, complete with three balconies, a kitchen, living room, and dining room. I suspected that I would never spend the evening at such a place again. Eddie wanted to go back out for a night cap.

So, we went to The Sandbar and Kitchen, a spot five miles north on A1A. In normal circumstances, Eddie would have used A1A to break into the lyrics of the Vanilla Ice song, "Ice

Ice Baby." He loved to find clever ways of taking a topic at hand in particular words and linking those words to song lyrics.

"Hey Matty, you know there's a song called A1A?" he'd say.

"How does it go?" I'd ask, playing along.

Then he would break into a chorus.

But not today.

Eddie was distraught. He was a little drunk, too. Eddie opened the car door and began walking toward the blue and white painted stucco restaurant that stood at the edge of the beach.

"Eddie, you forgot your mask," I reminded him. And I pulled out some spares from my box in the center console.

We elected to sit at the outdoor bar for dinner and drinks rather than waiting twenty minutes for the next available table. The black haired dark eyed bartender approached us asking, "Do you like cold beer?" he asked.

"Of course," answered Eddie. "What do you recommend?"

"I personally like a nice cold Warsteiner, but unfortunately we don't carry those."

The bartender, like Eddie, seemed to be quite the character. He wore a light-gray bandana backwards like one of the bad guys in an old country western who robs the bank.

"What are your names?"

"I'm Matt and this is Eddie, what's yours?"

"I'm Steve."

"Can I call you Stevo?" asked Eddie.

"You can call me whatever you want as long as you pay the check, behave yourself, and leave me a nice tip."

We ordered a couple of American Blonde Ales brewed locally in Fernandina Beach by First Love. After a couple of rounds, Eddie started acting more like himself.

"What brings you fellas down here in the middle of the pandemic?" asked Stevo.

"We drove down from Atlanta to get a way for a while and to scope out some investment opportunities."

"You guys are high rollers then, right? What kind of investment did you have in mind?"

"Correction. Eddie is looking at vacation homes, not me."

"What kind of work are you men in?"

"I'm a sportswriter for a local Atlanta newspaper and Eddie's a corporate lawyer."

"That explains it. He makes the big money. What was your name again?"

"My name is Matt Brusco," I answered. Stevo had never heard of me, but he and Eddie seemed to have a kindred connection. Both men were complete extroverts and outspoken in the way they carried on casual conversations with complete strangers. A stranger sitting at the bar may arrive at the impression that Stevo and Eddie had known each other for years. Both smiled in a contagious way that enticed others around them to smile.

"What do you think about properties in the Ft. Lauderdale area?" Eddie asked Stevo.

"Don't get me wrong. It's nice south of here, but Ft. Lauderdale is growing quickly and becoming more congested. I guess it depends on what you are looking for and your price range."

"I would love to have more of a small beach town feel than something that is littered with tourists. At the same time, my aim is to be far enough south that it's warm in the winter. I am thinking that 70 degrees would be ideal."

"That pretty much rules out this area then. Pompano Beach might be interesting for you."

"That's actually where we were headed."

Stevo looked at Eddie and gave him one final piece of advice. "Just remember, every penny has its consequence."

"What exactly does that mean?"

"You know it's like Benjamin Franklin said."

"Benjamin Franklin said, 'A penny saved is a penny earned,'" said Eddie.

"Bingo Eddie. See, if you spend your pennies on a bad investment there will be a consequence."

Stevo and Eddie matched wits for the next forty-minutes. What can be more entertaining than having a front row seat where a lawyer and bartender explore life's deepest philosophical debates? A sportswriter, a lawyer, and a priest walk into a bar . . .

Up to that point, we lacked the priest. When Father Murphy walked in, the joke was complete.

"Hey Father, can I get you the usual?" asked Stevo.

"Yes, my son," answered Father Murphy. "You know me too well."

Stevo removed a bottle of Macallan scotch from the top shelf and poured father a glass.

"That one is on me, Father. Hey Stevo, pour one for yourself and me too. Sorry Matty, you have to drive."

In between their second and third glass of scotch, Eddie confessed to the priest.

"Hey father, I need to make a confession."

In a deep Irish accent, Father Murphy responded, "I'm happy to hear your confession Eddie, but this is not the right time or place."

"Father, I impregnated my girlfriend Daisy, and we are not married."

Father Murphy tried to stop him, but Eddie continued. "And she lost the baby. Is God trying to punish us for this sin?"

Things went silent in the bar for a while.

"My son, God loves all of his children and wants what is best for them. Only God knows his will for his children, not I."

From that point on, things lightened up. Eddie's drunken confession seemed to liberate him from his guilt and pain. I assumed the top-end Macallan also played a role. Eddie looked at Stevo then back to Father Murphy.

"Father, can I ask you a personal question?"

"What would you like to know, my son?"

"Does God love Scotland more than Ireland?"

"Of course, not my son. Why do you ask such a question?"

"I find it interesting that the scotch from Scotland tastes better than the Irish whiskey. Otherwise, I would suspect that an Irish priest would not order Macallan instead of Jameson."

Father Murphy let out a boisterous laugh. Stevo looked on anxiously, waiting to see what the priest would come back with.

"Eddie my son, let me now ask you a question."

"Shoot."

"Do you think God discriminates against his creation?" asked Father Murphy.

"No, of course not."

"That's right, Eddie. Are Macallan and Jameson not both creations of God?"

Eddie nodded.

"Stevo, to show my friend Eddie that I do not discriminate either, please pour us each a glass of the finest Irish whiskey in the house. This one's on me, Eddie."

Father Murphy tossed back his shot to the laughter of everyone sitting around the bar.

As I watched the happy scene, I thought about the father's comment about God having an individual will for each of us. What was the will for Eddie and Daisy's baby, Mia, that never entered this world? Something about Mia's death seemed unfair to me. Any and every earthly experience she could have had, she never would. I thought deeply about a childhood acquaintance of mine. For the life of me, I cannot recall his name. I only remember that our mothers were close friends. The young boy was about the same age as me. He had muscular dystrophy which confined him to a wheelchair. I have vivid memories of seeing him sit in his wheelchair across the room. He watched my brothers and me play sports, and to this day I still feel guilty that he could not participate in our physical activities. My brothers and I tried to involve him in our activities, but he usually declined, preferring to watch from a distance. Those were my last memories of him.

A year after his life intersected with mine, his mother passed away from leukemia. The doctors gave her three months to live and accurately predicted her lifespan. Within three months of the diagnosis, she passed away. I later learned that the boy died sometime after his mother.

I recollect what I hoped to be true when I was thirteen or fourteen years old. I wished that the reason some people's lives were physically limited and shortened was because of their inherent goodness—that their pure hearts were being spared the rigors of life; I imagined, perhaps naively, that people who are innocent do not need to experience the highs and lows of life. That at least explained why the young boy and his mother's lives ended at such young ages.

Maybe that idea would be comforting to Eddie, maybe not. I am no expert on navigating through the stages of grief. For all I knew, Stevo and Father Murphy's light-heartedness had opened the door for Eddie to speak more openly about his story. Could the insignificant other principle apply to Eddie, Stevo, and the priest? Did Stevo and Father Murphy play an ever so slight role in entering Eddie's life in arguably one of the most challenging times? I likened the appearance of these complete strangers in our personal orbits to comets that burst into the sky, briefly lighting up the cosmos before quickly fading into darkness.

Eddie and I arrived back at the Ritz by around ten o'clock in the evening. I feared the night would not end well for him. He used me as a crutch as we passed through the lobby to the elevator. I was completely exhausted from a long day of driving and looked forward to falling into a deep peaceful sleep. Before doing so, I forced Eddie to hydrate. He reeked of stale beer, scotch, and whiskey. The full impact of his drunk would not set in until the next morning.

***

The rising sun over the Atlantic cast brilliant orange rays which stretched downward from the sky to the turquoise surface of the ocean. Eddie snored on while I went out onto the balcony to enjoy the sunrise.

After thirty minutes or so, I resolved to take a long morning run. I headed to Peters Point Park, which was a short distance from the Ritz. The six-plus mile paved trail wound alongside A1A, and the canopy of trees provided shade from the overhead sun. When I returned to the room to check on Eddie, he was still snoring away. So, I showered and went to fetch two coffees from the cafe downstairs.

Eddie looked like he had been hit by a train when I returned to the room.

"Good morning Eddie. I guess I don't need to ask you how you are feeling?"

"It's that obvious?"

"Yes, I do have this for you, but there is water in the fridge if you prefer."

"Thanks, Matty. I'll start with the coffee."

For a moment, I guiltily gave thanks that I wasn't Eddie that morning. We departed the hotel a little after noon and began the five-hour drive heading south on I-95 toward Pompano Beach. We stopped at McDonald's to pick up a chocolate shake for Eddie. Eddie slept the next four hours, waking up around the time we were nearing Port St. Lucie. Both of us were starving at this point, so we stopped at Shucker's on the Beach in Jensen Beach.

The break in the late afternoon created a relaxing atmosphere. Eddie looked at the menu on his iPhone using the newly popular application which shows the menu after the camera scrolls over the QR code or quick response coded icon. We patiently sat on the wooden deck under the shade of an umbrella until the server arrived. Eddie must have been starving because he ordered two separate types of fish tacos, Shrimp and Grouper. I followed him but selected grilled Mahi tacos instead. Neither one of us talked much throughout lunch. Shockingly, Eddie still had room for the key lime pie after his double taco order. I ordered a coffee, knowing that we needed to drive another hour and half before arriving at the Pompano Beach Marriott.

Eddie's hangover seemed to be coming around, until he passed back out as we merged onto I-95 South. By evening, we were checked into a new room in Pompano Beach, where we'd agreed to meet Eddie's real estate agent the next morning.

The next morning, the real estate agent picked us up in her blue Jaguar F-PACE. Eddie and the agent chatted about the local housing market and the pros and cons of the different coastal cities along the Gulf and Atlantic coasts. I tuned them out, looking out the window at all the luxury homes we drove by.

For the next three hours we toured every imaginable type of property that could be conceived as an investment. After walking through condos, standalone homes, and cottages, I felt completely drained. There was no way I could do this with Eddie for another two days. I reached my limit after three hours and about eight different properties. Eddie on the other hand looked as happy as a clam. I was relieved when the agent dropped us off at a restaurant near the Pompano Beach Pier called Oceanic.

"So Matty, what do you think?"

The last thing I wanted to do was to tamp down his excitement, so I worked hard to downplay my lack of enthusiasm for the house hunting process.

"This is a beautiful place, and there are certainly many good options for you to choose from."

"Matty, you don't have to pretend to like this. I could tell after visiting the second condo that you were ready to check out. You don't have to go with me tomorrow."

"Thanks. It's great that you are so passionate about this but honestly, it's just not for me."

"I know. Matty, I want to thank you. The past few days have been terribly difficult for me, as you probably know. Your willingness to drive me down here and to listen to me means a lot."

"It's really my pleasure. I have absolutely no idea of what you must be going through. I just want to help in any way that I can."

"You have. Somewhere along my drunken journey I let go. I cannot explain how the burden fell off my shoulders but somehow it did."

"Perhaps it was the combination of the priest and the whiskey."

"Maybe, who knows? I think just getting away from Atlanta and giving myself some space to process everything made the difference. Now I just want to be there for Daisy. We talked last night, and she is going to come down here with me."

"You're not coming back with me?"

"Matty, I will be back eventually, but I decided today that I want to buy something, and since I'm working remotely, Daisy and I will ride out the pandemic down here. You are not getting rid of me so fast. I still need a ride back to Atlanta to pick up Daisy and pack up my things."

"I'm going to miss you, Eddie."

"I will miss you too, Matty."

After we finished eating, I wanted to be alone, so I made up an excuse about having to make a few work calls. I hated lying to Eddie, but I desperately needed some time by myself to process everything. I never grasped the reality of how our lives were changing until Eddie shared his plans. The pandemic established a physical separation between my best friend and me, but now our relationships and next stages of life were creating a more permanent divide. I spent the better part of the last five years with Eddie. We evolved from being simply roommates to best friends. The moment Eddie informed me of his plans to temporarily relocate to Florida, I knew that our separation would go beyond geographic boundaries. In a short period of time, Lana and I would be married, and Eddie was well along the way to building a long-lasting relationship with Daisy.

I held my shoes in my hand while walking in the surf towards Pompano Beach Pier. Once I reached the pier, I sat down in the sand, looking out through the supporting wooden beams that held the weight of the boardwalk. Looking through the tunnel-shaped pier infrastructure created the illusion of gazing into my future, with miles and miles of open ocean in front of me. I thought more about how significant a role Eddie had played in my life.

He would never be considered an insignificant other.

Eddie and I started our long journey back to Atlanta a few days later. He managed to secure a six-month lease on a little beach cottage just north of Pompano Beach. We made the most of our road trip, reminiscing about our most memorable times. Neither of us touched upon the future and how that future would be inherently different than in the past. The subject was too raw.

We decided to stop in to see Stevo one more time once we reached Amelia Island. Father Murphy never showed up, but we enjoyed some great laughs with the bartender. A day and half later we were back in Atlanta. I dropped Eddie off at the Eclipse and said goodbye. We understood this was a real goodbye, but we avoided saying so to one other. I felt alone driving north on Georgia 400, but looked forward to reuniting with Lana.

I DO

The Trangate family had become immersed in 1980s television and movies in my absence. COVID restrictions created many unique opportunities to explore areas of interest that had either waned or never existed. The summer of 2020 felt more like the summer of 1988, with the Trangate family consuming episodes of *Alf*, *Growing Pains*, and *Family Ties*. They did not stop with television shows. They also enjoyed the movie blockbusters like *Coming to America*, *Big*, and the *Great Outdoors*.

On rare occasions I would join the family for the 1980s bonding sessions, but work consumed most of my time in the late summer. I preferred dedicating my free time to hanging out with Lana or writing my novel. The main upside to travel restrictions was more time and space to write.

I worked to avoid the political noise of the 2020 Presidential election, not caring which geriatric candidate the country would wind up selecting in November. People were losing their loved ones daily and others were losing their jobs or being laid off. The sweeping pandemic continued to destroy many lives in its path. I managed through the stress-filled days of confinement by running daily and then taking breaks to go out on long walks.

I missed Eddie already.

Lana returned to her firm (remotely) with a hero's welcome for her undercover role. All Lana's dreams were coming true. Raj and Kim promoted her to junior partner, but it took several weeks to extract the celebratory news from her. Always the modest one, she hesitantly communicated her promotion. I remember the conversation well. We were grilling dinner at the side of the pool and Lana had this glow. She smiled and I pried.

"You must have some good news, Lana."

She laughed. "Why did you say that?"

"Because for the past several days, you have had this huge smile on your face."

"Matty, maybe it's because I'm so in love with this boy and his long dirty blonde unkempt hair, beautiful hazel eyes, and slender yet athletic runner's body."

"No Lana, your radiating glee goes far beyond me. So, what is it?"

"Ok, Raj and Kim gave me a promotion."

"Congratulations! You of all people certainly deserve it."

"Thanks."

"This must be some promotion, because when I get promoted, I do not experience quite the same level of excitement that you have."

"It's sort of a big career jump. They made me a junior partner."

"Congratulations. So how do you plan to celebrate this momentous achievement of yours?"

Lana's tone shifted from playful to serious. "That is something I wanted to discuss with you."

I took a breath.

"Matty, along with the higher-level position, my salary and benefits increased considerably."

"That's fantastic!"

"Yes, but now I have the opportunity to do something I always intended to do, but . . . see, ever since I traveled to Ghana, I always hoped to start a nonprofit for young women immigrants. The two things that most break my heart are young women who are trafficked and those that never get a chance at getting an education."

"I think you should follow your dreams and take on the challenges that tear your heart to pieces."

"Thanks, Matty. I wanted to make sure you were on board, because soon it's not just me, but us."

"Of course, I fully support you and your choices."

"There is one thing, Matty. I do not have the time or energy to do this on my own, but I think I know someone who would be great in leading this role and being the director."

"I do too."

"Daisy," we said in unison.

Lana took no time jumping into the details of learning how to start a nonprofit. She diligently began the process of completing the paperwork. Lana filed the articles of incorporation, completed the state forms, and filed for tax-exempt status. Lucky for me, she completed this alone. I cannot fathom working on writing compliance requirements and drafting by-laws. I approached Eddie with the idea, which he not only fully endorsed, but he also decided to make a significant monetary contribution. Together, Lana and Eddie pitched the nonprofit to Daisy, who felt honored to be considered for the director role.

Despite her recent career success and starting up her future non-profit, I sensed something eating at Lana. Then one day I discovered what was weighing her down.

There was a gentle knock on the soft brown wooden barn office door. I stood up from the desk and walked over to slide open the door. Lana stood in the framed door opening with tears running down her cheeks. I embraced her at once. A few minutes later she stepped back and took my hands into hers. Lana looked deeply into my eyes.

"Matty, I cannot do this anymore."

I started to fear something terrible was coming next after hearing those words. What could be causing Lana such hurt or pain and what could she no longer do? I struggled to ground myself from thinking about the worst-case scenarios. The mind tends to steer towards the cliff rather than away from it once negative information is received.

"Lana, what is it that you can no longer do?"

"I cannot continue to live here with my parents. I want to get married."

I had never been so relieved in my life. Getting married sooner rather than later was better than the alternative of not marrying Lana at all.

"I'm in, Lana. I would love to get married as soon as we can. What's wrong?"

"Ever since I was a little girl, I dreamed of getting married at the Greek Orthodox."

"Right. Is there an issue with that now?"

"Matty, I talked to them, and with COVID restrictions and scheduling, the soonest we can get married there is early next year."

"And you definitely do not want to wait until then?"

"No, and it breaks my heart, because I always dreamed about getting married in the church I grew up attending."

"Lana, if getting married in the church is that important, we can wait a little longer."

"Matty, I just don't know what to do."

I still could not understand what upset her so much. Then I found the reason.

Lana grew up as the model child, always respecting her parents and acquiescing to their wishes. She never caused them any stress. Lana sailed through elementary, middle, and high school, always graduating with high honors at the top of her class. She always stayed out of trouble. I never really pondered the details of Lana's past, but looking at the present situation provided new insights. Lana is a people pleaser. She always puts the needs of others ahead of her own. That was clearly the case with going undercover for her firm. If her parents or brothers needed something, she dropped everything to address their requests.

"Set aside your commitment to the Greek church and your natural inclination to do what your parents desire," I said. "When and where do you want to get married?"

"I'd love to get married now with nothing more than a small intimate ceremony on the beach somewhere in Florida."

"What is stopping you?"

"Nothing, I guess, but my parents."

"The wedding is about you and only you."

"Well, I hope you know it's about you too," she added.

"Let's do it then. Let's get married as soon as we can get the dates booked."

"Matty, you know that I hate spontaneity."

"Yes, I know. Did you have any place in mind?"

"I was thinking about Fort Walton Beach, but what about your family? Do you think they can make it?"

"Yes, everyone is locked down, so I think they should be able to plan their schedules accordingly."

Lana did most of the wedding planning while I covered the Braves, who by September looked to be World Series bound. We intentionally scheduled the wedding during Thanksgiving week to account for the potential of the Braves playing in the 2020 World Series. The Braves clinched the National League East on September 22. Lana understood the nature of my job, which became all-consuming by late September.

Things were certainly on the up and up.

I could never have predicted how great the year of 2020 would have turned out for me personally. As with most of the world, everything seemed bleak in March. Then with each passing month, life found a way. Starting with baseball opening day, followed by Lana's acquittal, and now to top things off, I was covering the Braves on their march toward the World Series. Most importantly, I looked forward to marrying the woman of my dreams a short month and half later.

The roller coaster ride of life took a downturn after the Braves lost to the Dodgers in a seven-game series, which effectively ended their 2020 season on October 18. I had one simple task to complete before the wedding. The only assignment Lana gave me was to plan the honeymoon. I arrived at the idea of having a Florida peninsula honeymoon. The concept was to start the honeymoon in Fort Myers then drive east along the coast, hugging the shoreline and spending a night or two at a nice resort. We would spend the first night in Fort Walton then proceed to St. Petersburg Treasure Island. From there we would make additional stops along the Gulf Coast at Sanibel Island then Marco Island. Our next destination would be Key West, where I hoped to spend a few days. I always wanted to visit Hemmingway's home and I hoped to gain some inspiration there for my novel. From the Keys, we would travel on to the east coast along the Atlantic. The idea was to stop at Pompano Beach then move north to Hutchinson Island. I planned on making Amelia Island our last destination. Who knows? Maybe Lana and I could have a drink with Father Murphy while Stevo tended bar?

Lana and I were married on November 21, 2020. Our closest family and friends joined us on a warm late fall evening at sunset. I stood about thirty feet away from where the emerald Gulf of Mexico waves broke along the white powdery sand of Fort Walton beach. Just as Lana planned, she walked down the sand escorted by her father, while Pachelbel's "Canon in D" played softly in the background. Lana looked breathtakingly beautiful as she glided down the sands in her long white dress. A local family friend and pastor named Gilbert performed our wedding ceremony. The local Destin pastor reminded of a younger Mr. Romero, with a gigantic laugh.

Lana and I exchanged our *I Do's* and concluded with the traditional kiss.

We took what seemed like several hours' worth of wedding photos along the beach where I discovered the only thing worse than wearing a tuxedo was having a tuxedo filled with sand. Lana must have recognized that I was slowly approaching the expiration time for wearing dress clothes. "It's ok Matty," she whispered. "I can see your Cinderella moment has arrived. Go ahead and change into your blue jeans and old-gray t-shirt."

"Lana, are you serious?"

"Yes, my husband. Besides, pictures of you in your casual wear and me in my wedding dress will make for a great story."

I excused myself while Lana mingled with the guests at the local dive bar, where we would celebrate our reception. Our first dance would take place on the beach to Matt Nathanson's "All We Are."

I felt like I was living out the lyrics. The night was perfect. I could not have dreamed of something so beautiful. This was one of the moments in life where I hoped time would freeze. I wanted to stay in that place and state of mind indefinitely. I knew the future will certainly bring unforeseen challenges, but there is no one on earth I would rather be with than Lana in the toughest of circumstances. The love of my life. My wife and partner.

My significant one.

ABOUT THE AUTHOR

Brian currently lives in Milton, Georgia, with his wife Irene and their two sons. *Insignificant Ones* is his second novel following his debut novel, *+ One*. He is also the author of several non-fiction books, including *Generational Lessons from Dad* and *Fifty Half's from First to Last*.

Made in the USA
Columbia, SC
09 August 2021